STORM COUNTRY

Also by Deanna Madden

Helena Landless

Gaslight and Fog

The Haunted Garden (a novella)

The Wall

Forbidden Places

The World Beyond: A Novel of Ancient Greece

The Box

STORM COUNTRY

DEANNA MADDEN

FLYING DUTCHMAN PRESS

ISBN 978-0-5785-7166-9

Cover design by SelfPubBookCovers.com/Shardel

Flying Dutchman Press

2019

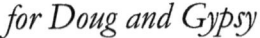

for Doug and Gypsy

CHAPTER 1

He picked up his binoculars again and trained them on the young woman sunning herself on the lonely stretch of beach. A trickle of sweat ran down the side of his face. He had been watching her for well over an hour. She was lying on her stomach on a yellow towel, propped on her elbows, a book open in front of her—a pretty young woman in a white bikini, tanned, long-legged, and slim.

It was the second day he had staked out this site, waiting for her to appear and hoping that when she did, someone suspicious looking might approach her—a drug dealer, a smuggler, or some other shady character—but so far she had lain there reading her book uninterrupted. Apparently she liked having the spot to herself, her only company an occasional gull that landed on the sand and pecked idly about, then flew off again with a squawk as the surf rolled in and broke against the shore.

She might have been any twenty-something, although most young women her age would have spread their towels farther up the beach where the volleyball crowd gathered and the joggers and windsurfers hung out. She appeared to have chosen this strip of sand deliberately, as if she preferred being alone. Maybe she did, but it was also an ideal location for an illegal transaction conducted away from prying eyes, and so he was disappointed when no one at all showed up.

She was a looker. Too bad she was involved with Carlos Ruiz and his gang. He didn't know how deeply, but the federal agent who had told him about her had warned him not to trust her. All he knew about her was her name—Sofia Ramirez—and that she was from Mexico, but even that much might not be true. The federal agent had hinted she could be one of Ruiz's illegals from Central America, smuggled across the border and set up with false papers. Ruiz was well known to immigration authorities but hard to pin anything on, an ex-con who had done time for drug dealing and petty theft but was probably guilty of worse.

He stretched, trying to work a cramp out of his leg after crouching there too long. So far no one had paid any attention to him—not the old man walking his dachshund, or the two teenaged boys who were jogging, or the young couple with a picnic basket looking for a likely place to spread their feast. If challenged, he would claim to be birdwatching—maybe not a very convincing cover story, but one that would explain the binoculars he hoped.

Glancing at his watch, he saw it was almost three o'clock. Doubtful anyone would show up now. They hadn't yesterday and probably wouldn't today. He couldn't keep surveilling the girl with nothing to show for it. Time was running out. By the end of the week he would have to get back to Denver. If he couldn't catch her in the act of doing something illegal—which is what the feds were hoping for—maybe he could find out something by talking to her. After all, she was the only lead he had as to what had happened to his friend Eric.

He stood, brushed the sand off his jeans, and slipped the binoculars into his backpack. Seeing them might spook her. Bad enough that there wasn't another soul in sight on the beach. Well, that couldn't be helped. He slid his arms into the straps of the backpack and jogged down to the water's edge to make it look more natural when he appeared—as if he were walking along the shore and had come upon her by accident.

She didn't look up as he neared. Either she was deeply engaged in her book or she was ignoring him.

When he was opposite her, he stopped and called out, "Nice day, isn't it?"

Her head turned and she stared at him. Her face was surrounded by a mass of dark curls. The waves kept rolling in, crashing, and sending water slithering up the sand and over his toes. He had rolled up the bottoms of his jeans to keep them from getting wet.

"You from here?" he asked, trying to sound friendly. He wanted her to see him as a harmless guy-next-door type. He grinned and squinted toward where the Gulf met the horizon in a pale blue line, then glanced back at the girl.

She was watching him with big dark wary eyes, looking as if she might bolt at any second. He would have to talk fast if he didn't want to lose what might be his only chance to make contact.

"I only ask because I'm not from here," he said, hastening on. "I'm from out of town. Just here for some R&R. Maybe you could steer me toward a good restaurant—or nightspot?

Where do folks around here go to have some fun when the sun goes down?"

He thought she might answer La Roca, which was the bar Ruiz owned farther up the coast. In fact, he was hoping she would answer that, but she stayed silent. She sat up slowly and put on sunglasses, hiding her eyes. He tried again. As long as he could keep her there, he might be able to learn what she knew about the disappearance of Eric. He figured she might know something since she was Carlos Ruiz's girlfriend, but he needed to proceed cautiously and not scare her off.

"By the way, I'm Mark. And you are . . . ?"

He hardly expected this opening gambit to work, but it did.

"Sofia." Her voice was almost drowned out by the crash of the surf, but she had given him the opening he needed, and so he plunged on, encouraged.

"You come here often, Sofia?"

She shrugged a bare shoulder. "Sometimes."

"Nice spot."

"The Reef."

"I beg your pardon?"

"You asked where to go. The Reef. They have good seafood." With the sudden rush of words there was no mistaking her Spanish accent.

"Oh, right. Thanks. What about you? Are you doing anything later tonight? Want to join me for dinner?" It was too fast, but he had to chance it. He might not get another shot.

"I can't."

"Why not?" He gave her his most winning grin.

She looked at the horizon and then back. "I have to work."

Keep her talking, he told himself.

"What time do you get off?" He gave her another grin, trying to look as harmless as possible. Just a guy on a beach trying to pick up a good-looking girl. If he could get her to say yes, it might be the break he needed.

But apparently she was done answering his questions. She stood up, slipped on a white cover-up as if suddenly self-conscious and in one deft movement swept up the yellow beach towel and flung it over her arm. In a few more minutes she would be gone and his opportunity lost.

"Sorry. I didn't mean to scare you off."

She reached for her bag. "You aren't scaring me off. It's time for me to go."

"I don't suppose you'd consider giving me your phone number?" he asked.

The sunglasses stared at him blankly. Then she gestured vaguely down the beach. "Just keep walking. There are more girls down there. If you're lucky, maybe you'll find your dinner date."

"Wait," he said as she turned to leave. "If you won't give me your number, how about I give you mine?"

She looked back, puzzled. "Why? What would be the point?"

By now he had whipped the business card out of his jeans pocket—the one he had made for just such an occasion that said his name was Mark Anderson and he was a software engineer in Denver.

He held it out at arm's length as he closed the distance between them, moving slow so as not to alarm her. She took the card and glanced at it, a small frown furrowing her brow.

"Who knows?" he said. "Maybe you'll change your mind."

"I don't think so."

But she dropped the card into her beach bag along with her book before she walked away, trudging through the sand in flip-flops, headed back toward the parking lot, where he knew her beat-up black Ford pickup waited. He didn't follow her. It would have looked too suspicious and undone all his effort to gain her trust.

That evening when he walked into La Roca, she was working behind the bar. She wore black slacks and a black shirt open at the neck with the glint of a tiny gold cross at her throat, her hair pulled back in a ponytail. Her eyes widened when she saw him, then slid past as if she hadn't recognized him.

Most of the tables were taken, but there were a couple of stools open at the bar. He slid onto one of them and glanced casually around the crowded room. Ruiz was huddled with two other men at a nearby table with several bottles of beer in front of them. He recognized him right away from the photo the federal agent had shared with him. They seemed to be discussing something important, judging by the serious expressions on their faces. He would have liked to get close enough to hear what they were saying, but even if he managed to snag a chair at the closest table, the noise level was too high to hear anything. Mariachi music blasted from the speaker system while a soccer game blared from the TV above the bar and customers shouted to be heard over the din. Add in the clink of glasses and bottles and the cumulative effect was near deafening.

Two young women were on duty—Sofia and a petite dark-haired girl waiting tables. He waited patiently for Sofia to come to him. Since he was sitting at the bar, she couldn't just ignore him. When she finally wandered over, her expression carefully neutral, she asked what he wanted, not meeting his eyes. He ordered a beer.

"You should leave," she said in a low voice, leaning forward so only he would hear. He caught a whiff of the scent she wore. It reminded him of roses.

"Why?"

"I don't know why you're here, but you should leave. *Now.*"

"But I just got here."

The man on the barstool beside him—a tall lanky fellow with glazed eyes riveted on the flat screen TV above the bar—let out a cheer at that moment. Evidently his soccer team had just scored a goal.

Sofia slipped away before he could say anything else. While he waited for her to bring his beer, he scanned the room again. It was a mostly Hispanic crowd, many of whom seemed to know each other. His eye passed over Ruiz again. No mistaking the scar on the side of his face or the tattoo of a viper on his neck. His arms were covered with tattoos. In fact, scarcely an inch of skin remained unmarked except for his face. Some dangerous men didn't look dangerous. Ruiz did. It could be fatal to underestimate a man like that. He would have to be careful if he didn't want to end up like Eric, who was probably dead.

Soon the girl was back. She slid his beer toward him. "Leave," she said in a low voice, her eyes locked on his. They were brown and gorgeous, dark pools a man could drown in. "You don't belong here. Turn around right now while you still can and leave."

"Why?" he said, feigning innocence. "I haven't had time to drink my beer."

Her eyes flicked around the room, taking in Ruiz, still deep in conversation with his two companions. "I don't know how you found me, but I thought I made myself clear. *Not interested.*" She talked fast, rocketing through her words, but there was no mistaking her meaning.

"Whoa," he said. "You think I'm here because of earlier when we met on the beach? Seriously, I had no idea you worked here. I came because someone told me it was a nice place to grab a beer."

She narrowed her eyes, skeptical.

Suddenly Ruiz was standing at his elbow. "Is there a problem?"

"No, no problem," he said, shaking his head. "Just a friendly conversation."

"Is he giving you trouble?" Ruiz asked the girl.

"No, it's okay. He was just leaving."

"A friend of yours?" He kept his eyes on the girl, not sparing a glance at the man on the barstool.

"No, I've never seen him before." She met Ruiz's stare straight on, steel against steel.

The people near them had gone still. The man watching the soccer game got unsteadily to his feet and lurched away in the direction of the men's room. Maybe he just needed to relieve himself, or maybe he saw it was a good time to make himself scarce.

"I think you should leave," Ruiz said without looking at him. "You're bothering the lady."

"I was just trying to ask her for a date," he said with a smile. "You know how it is. A pretty girl—"

"She's my wife."

That stopped him cold. Now he knew one more thing about her. She hadn't mentioned that she was married. Nor had the federal agent.

Well, this was awkward.

"Sorry." It was all he could think of to say under the circumstances.

"Carlos—" the girl began.

Before she could say more, a fist slammed into his face. Somewhere nearby a woman screamed. There was a scraping of chairs as people sprang to their feet. His arms were pinned behind him by men he couldn't see. Ruiz grinned at him before he hit him again. And then someone hit Ruiz and all hell broke loose.

CHAPTER 2

You sure about this?" Teresa asked as they struggled together, each under one of the man's arms, to steer him away from La Roca as fast as they could. He seemed dazed by the blow Carlos had landed and his nose was bleeding. Other people spilled out of the bar and hurried past them, running for their cars to escape before the police arrived.

"No, but I couldn't just leave him there," Sofia said.

"Why not?"

"Carlos might kill him."

"Couldn't you just explain that you don't know him?"

"I did." She turned her head toward the man. "Which car?" she demanded in English.

"The white Nissan." He pointed with an unsteady finger.

She saw it, near the rock that gave the bar its name. Fortunately it wasn't far. With Teresa's help, she maneuvered him into the front passenger seat. She noticed the new car smell and the empty back seat. Obviously a rental.

"No," he said, struggling to get back out. "I can drive."

"No, you can't," she said, blocking the way. "Key?" She

held out her hand. "And hurry. The cops will be here any minute."

As if to confirm her words, they heard sirens approaching.

He reached into his jeans pocket and pulled out the key fob. She snatched it from his hand, slammed the door, dashed around the car, and slid into the driver's seat. The engine leaped to life.

Teresa leaned down to look in through the open window, her eyes worried. "What if Carlos asks where you've gone?"

"Tell him you don't know," Sofia said.

"I can drive," the man said again.

She glanced at him. He had one eye rapidly swelling shut and blood dripping from his nose. She plucked a Kleenex from her pocket and shoved it in his hand. It wasn't much but it would have to do. They shot out of the parking lot just as the first police cruiser pulled in, its blue lights flashing and siren wailing. A second police cruiser followed close behind.

"Where are you staying?" she asked as they sped away.

"It's really not necessary for you to drive me back to my motel," he said, the Kleenex pressed to his nose. "If you'd just pull over . . ."

"I'm not going to pull over," she said in Spanish, then realized he couldn't understand her and repeated it in English.

He must have seen that she was determined to drive him back to his motel because he gave up arguing with her.

"The Alhambra," he said. "Do you know where it is?"

"Of course I know where it is." She frowned. "Why didn't you leave when I told you to?"

He ignored the question. "Is he always like that?"

"Sometimes worse." She was silent, remembering how Carlos had once threatened her with his knife, but he had been drunk at the time. Now she knew to stay away from him when he was drunk. Most of the time she got along with him. He let her do what she wanted, as long as she didn't give him a reason to complain. It could have been worse.

"You were an idiot to go there," she said. "Didn't you notice you were the only Anglo in the bar?"

"What? No, I didn't notice. Was I?" He dabbed at his nose. "I didn't see any signs saying Anglos keep out."

She swore under her breath in Spanish. Stupid gringo. How had he survived this long in the world? He was everything she despised. Typical pampered Anglo, privileged background, college education. He had no idea some people might hate him for that. What did he know of suffering? When had he had to worry about having enough food to eat or a roof over his head? Or being raped or beat up or killed? The world had handed him everything on a silver platter. Drop him down in a place like San Salvador and he wouldn't last half a day.

They passed through a stretch of commercial properties— gas stations, a car dealership, a mini mall. She cursed impatiently under her breath in Spanish whenever she had to stop for a red light. When she turned off on a road that ran along the coast, she relaxed a little. Traffic was lighter here. There were pockets of houses. Minutes later she swung the Nissan into the circular drive of the Alhambra, an old two-story motel painted pink that looked out on the moonlit water of the Gulf.

"Which room?"

"Behind the building. Number 21."

She drove around the building and slipped into a parking space near room number 21.

"How will you get back?" he asked.

"I'll call a friend to pick me up."

"All right. Well, thanks." He started to open his door.

Before he could get out, she jumped out and darted around to his side.

"I can take it from here," he said, waving her off, the balled up bloody Kleenex still pressed to his nose.

She held her hand out for his key card.

"No, really," he said. "I don't think you should come in."

She put her hands on her hips. "You go to all the trouble of tracking me down at La Roca and getting beat up, and now you don't want me to come in?"

"That was before I knew you had a homicidal maniac for a husband."

"Well, at least let me come in and pee."

He couldn't very well refuse her, not after she had helped him. She watched as he pulled out his keycard and then fumbled at the lock until he finally got it to release.

Once they were inside, she disappeared into the bathroom and came back a minute later with a wet washcloth.

"What are you doing?" he asked, eyeing the washcloth.

"Cleaning you up. You look like you were hit by a truck."

"Feels like it too," he said, sitting on the bed. "You might have warned me."

"I tried." She dabbed at his face.

"Ow, that hurts."

"Here. Hold it to your nose and put your head back till it stops bleeding."

"Why did you marry a man like that?" he asked as he lay back on the bed with the washcloth pressed to his nose.

"I didn't."

He gave her a look. "What? He's *not* your husband?"

She shrugged.

"Boyfriend?"

"You could say that. Why didn't you leave when I told you to?"

"It seemed like a nice place."

"Yeah. Right. All those nice friendly people."

She strolled restlessly around the room, flipping on light switches, pulling the curtains closed, looking in the nightstand drawer. She picked up the wallet he had just laid on the nightstand. "You should leave first thing tomorrow. It's not safe to stay here."

"Why? You think he'll come after me just because I was hitting on you? Isn't that kind of extreme?"

"Carlos is an extreme kind of guy."

"Yeah, I noticed."

"There are lots of other places to go for your R&R."

"Maybe I like this one."

"Who's Mark Judd?"

"*What?*" He raised his head and stared at her.

"I looked in your wallet." She held it up for him to see.

"Hey, who said you could look in my wallet?"

"Your driver's license says you are Mark *Judd*, not Mark Anderson like on that little card you gave me. So which is it? Judd or Anderson?"

He laid his head down again. "One is for my business."

She quirked an eyebrow. "And that would be?"

"Oh, for god's sake."

"Are you really here for R&R, as you call it?"

"Why else would I be here?"

Why indeed. She looked at him lying stretched out on the bed in his black T-shirt and jeans, his head propped up by two pillows. Good-looking, yes, but everything about him shouted trouble. She was not about to let her guard down. For all she knew he might be an undercover cop. Although that was unlikely given how clueless he seemed to be. Surely an undercover cop would not have walked into La Roca without backup.

The white washcloth was turning pink. If he got blood on the bed, the motel might not like it. Then again, motels had to overlook certain things if they wanted to keep their customers coming back. Blood on the bedding might be one of those.

"What about you?" he asked. "Why are you involved with a known felon like Ruiz?"

Her radar snapped on. "How did you know he was a felon?"

"Lucky guess."

"I owe him."

"For what?"

She straightened her back. "He helped me when no one else would."

"What—to cross the border?"

She inhaled swiftly. Until now she had assumed he was just a naive Anglo who had stumbled into something more dangerous than he realized, but maybe he was something else entirely. "Are you with immigration?"

"No."

"But you're not a software engineer, are you?"

When he didn't deny it, she went into the bathroom and splashed water on her face. How could she have been so stupid? Here she was thinking she was protecting him, and all the time he was probably with border patrol or immigration. She should have let Carlos beat him to a pulp.

In the mirror over the sink her reflection stared back at her like the face of a stranger. There were dark circles under her eyes. Wisps of hair had slipped loose from her ponytail. Would there ever be a time when she felt safe? A time when she didn't have to worry about being sent back to El Salvador? It had been only nine months since she crossed the border, but she felt a decade older. She couldn't go back. The gangs would kill her, just as they had killed almost everyone she cared about. She had nothing to go back to.

She felt calmer when she walked back into the room. He was lying on the bed staring at the ceiling, the washcloth pressed to his nose.

"Are you going to arrest me?" she asked.

"I told you, I'm not with immigration."

Maybe he wasn't, but she still didn't trust him. His walking into La Roca tonight was no accident. "Has the bleeding stopped?"

He lowered the washcloth and frowned at it. "I think so. God, what a mess. I wonder if my nose is broken."

"Here. Give it to me. I'll see if I can wash it out."

She took the washcloth into the bathroom and ran water over it, watching the blood wash away in pink rivulets, then left the washcloth to soak in cold water.

"So how did you get mixed up with Ruiz?" he asked when she returned.

She perched on a corner of the bed near his feet. He still had his shoes on. Big athletic shoes. Even the soles looked new. She sighed. "I told you. He helped me when no one else would."

"Crossing the border?"

She nodded. Why not? He had already guessed as much. "That and through Tamaulipas. It's cartel country. Very dangerous."

He looked at her, eyes narrowed. "Where exactly are you from?"

If he wasn't from immigration, what did it matter if she told him? "El Salvador."

"You made the journey on your own?"

"No. There were others." She tilted her head back and looked at the ceiling. There had been three of them at the start—Rosa, a year younger than her, fleeing an abusive husband; Maria, only thirteen, whose parents feared for her life because her brother's rival gang had threatened to kill her; and herself—four, counting her little boy. Later there were others that they joined up with.

"How does Ruiz fit into this?"

"He offered to help me and some of the others."

"For a price."

She felt a flicker of irritation. "Yes, for a price. There were gangs . . ." She stopped. It wasn't something she liked to talk about. Or think about. The gangs. The cartels. The corrupt police. Once Carlos and his men were escorting her, the gangs backed off. There was strength in numbers, especially when that included men with weapons. Carlos had told her he would take care of her and he had. What happened at the border wasn't his fault. She blamed it entirely on the Americans and their cruel laws. If she had known they would take Diego away from her, she would have found another way. She had thought once she got that far, they would be safe, but she was wrong.

"I should go now," she said, standing.

He pushed himself up on his elbows. "Are you sure it's safe to go back?"

"He won't hurt me."

"How can you be sure?"

"I just am."

She moved to the door.

"Sofia—"

She stopped, her hand on the doorknob, and turned her head.

He was looking at her. He had nice eyes. Yes, better to leave now. To stay longer would be a mistake. He wasn't someone she should get involved with. They came from different worlds. And there was Carlos to think of. She didn't dare take the risk.

"Be careful," he said.

Outside insects buzzed around the Alhambra's lighted entrance sign. It was a typical August night—hot and humid with a lazy saltwater breeze drifting in from the Gulf. She could hear the surf breaking on the shoreline. Overhead stars glittered like a million tiny jewels. The small blinking light of an airplane drifted across the sky. It was quiet and peaceful except for an

SUV that sped past with its windows down and a subwoofer blasting out a throbbing bass.

As she waited for Teresa, she thought uneasily about Carlos. She had told the Anglo he wouldn't hurt her, but she couldn't be sure of that. He could be violent. She had seen him kill a man in cold blood. He had said if she ever told, he would kill her, and she believed him.

But what choice did she have? There was no place else for her to go. With Carlos at least she had a roof over her head and food to eat. He even paid her to work in the bar. If she left him, how would she make ends meet? It wasn't like she could just snap her fingers and get another job. People only had to hear her accent to wonder if she was an illegal alien. Never mind the papers Carlos had given her. She wasn't sure they would hold up under scrutiny. And there was Diego to think about. If she wanted to get him back, she had to put up with Carlos. Like it or not, he was her best chance of getting her son back. On her own she was unlikely to persuade immigration authorities to return him. If she made a fuss, they could simply deport her, and there was nothing she could do about it.

What did the man she had just left know of such things? He lived in a world where he never doubted his right to belong. Apparently he had no child or wife to worry about. A girlfriend maybe. Men like him usually had girlfriends. Or wives. He said he was in town for some R&R. More likely looking for some action. Maybe he'd had a fight with his girlfriend. Or wife. Whatever his reason for coming to Mustang Island, if he was smart, he'd take her advice and go back home. Carlos wasn't someone to mess around with.

She just hoped he hadn't seen her and Teresa sneaking the Anglo out of La Roca. If he had, she was in trouble. She would have to think of a way to explain why she had helped the Anglo. It had been a stupid thing to do, but she had felt like it was a little bit her fault that he had showed up there. She shouldn't have spoken to him on the beach. She would have to be more careful in the future.

She was just beginning to wonder what was keeping Teresa when her friend roared up on her motorcycle.

"Did Carlos say anything?" Sofia asked.

"I told him I didn't see you leave." Teresa handed her a helmet.

"Thanks. I owe you," Sofia said as she strapped on the helmet and swung a leg over the back of the bike.

"What about the Anglo?"

"What about him?"

"Did he and you—you know?"

She lightly slapped Teresa's back. "Of course not."

"Why not? He's cute."

"Carlos would kill me."

Teresa waved a hand dismissively. "You wouldn't have to tell him."

"He'd know. Trust me."

When they pulled up a little later at La Roca, the bar was dark and the parking lot deserted. The sign in front was off. There was no light over the doorway, just the pole light in the parking lot. Apparently Carlos had closed the bar after the excitement earlier. Teresa pulled up beside Sofia's pickup, standing alone in the empty lot.

"Did anyone get arrested?" Sofia asked after she climbed off the motorcycle and removed the helmet.

"No, Carlos told the cops it was just a misunderstanding."

Sofia knew he had probably also slipped them some money. It was a sort of arrangement he had with them. He paid them and they looked the other way when incidents like tonight happened.

She said good-bye to Teresa and climbed into her pickup. It was a short drive up the road to the bungalow she shared with Carlos. The place wasn't much to look at, but she had gradually added a few touches in the nine months she had been living with him that made it feel more like a home—curtains at the windows, a crucifix on the wall, and a small geranium in a ceramic pot on the counter that she had bought on impulse at a hardware store.

When she walked in, Carlos was sprawled on the couch in front of the TV watching one of the *Fast and Furious* movies in Spanish. An empty beer bottle sat on the floor beside him.

"Where've you been?" he asked, his eyes glued to the screen.

"I went for a walk. I left when the fight broke out. Didn't really want to be around if the cops started arresting people."

"Things quieted down when they got there. Hey, did you see what happened to the Anglo sitting at the bar?"

"The one you punched?"

"Yeah." He smiled, remembering. "Did you see the look on his face?"

"Before or after you hit him?"

His smile widened, showing the gap where he had lost a tooth several years before in another fight. "Before. Did you see what happened to him? He seemed to just disappear. I got sidetracked and when I went back he was gone."

"He probably left."

"Yeah, that's what I figured. A real wimp. You sure you didn't know him?"

"Never saw him before in my life."

"You better not be lying to me."

"I'm not." She stared him down, knowing she must not show any sign of wavering. If she wavered, he would pounce.

"You know I'd kill you if I found out you'd been with another man," he said matter-of-factly.

She lifted her chin. "Then you'd have to find another bartender—one you'd have to pay more."

He rubbed his chin and chuckled. "Yeah, I suppose I would. But don't forget I'm the only one who can get your kid back."

She focused her eyes on the crucifix on the wall. Could he get Diego back? She was beginning to wonder. "When?" It had been a long day and she was tired. The word slipped out before she could stop it.

"I told you, babe. These things take time. You got to be patient."

"It's been nine months."

There was silence in which she could hear only the heightened tempo of the soundtrack for the movie he was watching.

"Come here."

It was a command, not an invitation. Every sense went on the alert. Reluctantly she moved closer, careful to keep her face expressionless. Better not to show fear. All she had to protect her was her ability to hide what she was feeling. If she showed fear, she would be at his mercy.

He stood up. He was a little taller than she was. There was a hint of a smile on his face, but that meant nothing. His hand shot out and grabbed her throat. Her heart was pounding, and her hands pried desperately at his fingers. Then just as suddenly he released her. Relief swept over her. He was just trying to scare her. She thought of the man she had seen him kill and remembered the flash of the knife and the quick thrust of his arm as he brought it down. The man had been tied to a chair. He had no chance to defend himself. The image was seared in her brain and she was never going to get it out.

"Have you forgotten it was me who saved you from that scum in Mexico?" Carlos asked.

"I haven't forgotten."

"You'd never have made it to the border without me. Just remember that."

She didn't answer. For Diego's sake, she had to restrain herself. She had lost everyone else. She couldn't lose him too. But more and more she doubted that Carlos could get him back for her. She suspected he dangled that in front of her to keep her from leaving. But since he was her best hope of getting her little boy back—maybe her only hope—she stayed and put up with his volatile moods and his temper. It wouldn't always be like this, she promised herself.

She touched her neck where his fingers had pressed. What if one of these days he went too far? What if he choked her to death or stabbed her in a fit of rage? If she disappeared, would anyone notice or care? What would happen to Diego then? She had to stay alive for his sake. He didn't have anyone else. If she couldn't get him back, he would grow up surrounded by strangers who would never love him as much as she did. For both their sakes she had to be strong.

CHAPTER 3

When Mark woke up, he felt awful. He dragged himself into the bathroom and flipped on the light over the mirror. Definitely a black eye. He touched it gingerly. Sore too. He was just sorry he hadn't gotten a chance to pay Ruiz back. He hadn't expected Ruiz's goons to grab him. Of course, you couldn't expect someone like Ruiz to fight fair. He hoped the girl didn't get in trouble for helping him. She had stuck her neck out when she must have known it was risky. All the same, he could have kicked himself for not trying to persuade her to stay longer. He hadn't been thinking clearly. That punch to the face must have affected him more than he realized at the time. Now he'd lost an opportunity to find out what she might know about Eric's disappearance. Maybe she didn't know anything, but he had a hunch she did.

So what next? He couldn't just walk into the bar and confront Ruiz, especially not after what happened last night. Chances were he would disappear like Eric had. And if he started asking questions, word would soon get back to Ruiz. But what other options did he have? None really. And time was running out. So that settled it. He would grab some breakfast and then start asking questions. No more wasting time hanging around the beach to surveil the girl.

He drove around for a while until he spotted a small cafe with outdoor tables that looked like a good place to have breakfast. After sitting down under a festive red umbrella, he soon was sipping his first coffee of the morning and digging into an omelet. As he ate, he surveyed his surroundings. Port Aransas was a pleasant little resort town on a barrier island on the Gulf. He couldn't see the water from where he was, but he knew it was nearby, almost within walking distance. You could smell the tang of saltwater in the air.

It was nice to be outdoors, sparrows twittering in the trees, a pigeon scavenging for scraps under the next table, cars speeding by as commuters hurried to work. An old man ambled past with his yellow mongrel dog that looked as old and worn out as he did. The girl who was waiting tables trotted out of the restaurant with a big smile and refilled his coffee.

"Looks like you ran into something," she said, referring to his black eye.

"Yeah, a pole."

"Bet you were on your phone."

"How'd you guess?"

"I twisted my ankle once stepping off a curb while I was texting. I try to pay more attention to curbs now. Well, give a holler if you need anything else."

As he sipped his coffee, a plan began to form in his mind. He would start by showing Eric's photo at businesses along the waterfront that rented boats or sold bait and ask if anyone had seen him. Maybe he would get lucky.

He was just finishing the omelet when a battered black pickup flew past. He had a glimpse of a young woman's intent face surrounded by a wild tangle of hair. She was looking straight ahead and didn't notice him sitting there. He recognized her immediately. Sofia Ramirez—the girl from the beach. Where was she off to in such a rush? If his car had been closer, he would have jumped in and followed her, but it was half a block away. She would be long gone by the time he got to it. But then as he watched, her pickup swung into a drive farther down the street and lurched to a stop. She bounded out and took off running. Now what was that all about? Curious, he decided to find out.

He hastily paid the girl who had waited on him, telling her to keep the change, then set off at a jog down the street. When he reached the drive where Sofia's pickup had turned, he saw it sitting in the parking lot of an old church with Spanish architecture and a statue of Mary standing in front. He was reluctant to follow her inside. She was not likely to be making a drug drop in a church, although maybe that was what would make it a perfect front for illegal drug activity. In any case he didn't feel comfortable following her into a place like that. It was too much like stalking, and besides he just wasn't crazy about going into a church. But maybe he would hang around for a bit to see if she came back out.

His patience was rewarded ten minutes later when she reappeared, looking troubled and frowning at the ground as she retraced her steps to her pickup. Not until she was almost to him did she look up and notice him standing there beside her truck. She stopped in her tracks and stared at him.

"What are you doing here? I thought you were going to leave." When she was stressed, she spoke faster and her accent was more noticeable.

"That was your idea, not mine." He smiled.

She glanced nervously at the passing traffic. "You can't stay here. If Carlos sees you, he'll have his men beat you up. Or beat you up himself. You're lucky all you got yesterday was a black eye. Next time you might not get off so easy."

"Let me worry about that."

She gave him a wary look. "Are you following me?"

"No, I was just having breakfast down the street and saw you drive by. Thought I'd say thank you for helping me get back to my motel last night."

She looked uncertainly in the direction he indicated as if trying to decide whether to believe him.

"If he's so dangerous, why do you stay with him?"

She gave a little shrug. "I have nowhere else to go."

"There must be some place . . ."

"There isn't." She cut him off so abruptly he thought it better not to pursue it. "Sorry about your black eye," she added.

"Why should you be sorry? You weren't the one who hit me."

Her eyes flicked to the street, then back. "What can I say to make you go away? I don't even know why you're here. Are you a cop?"

"No." He understood her distrust of the law. She had as much as confessed to being an illegal the night before.

"What then?"

He pulled out his wallet with the photo of Eric. "Have you ever seen this man?"

She took the photo and looked at it, then quickly handed it back. "No, who is he?"

"A friend."

"No, I've never seen him before." She pushed her hair out of her eyes but didn't meet his gaze.

He was pretty sure she was lying. How could he persuade her to tell him what she knew?

"No one's heard from him for three weeks now. He came to Port Aransas to investigate your boyfriend and disappeared. I'm here to find out what happened to him."

She frowned again. "I thought you said you weren't a cop."

"I'm not."

"Then why are you asking all these questions?"

"I told you. He's a friend."

"I can't tell you anything."

"But you saw him?"

She shook her head. "I have to go."

"He has a family. A wife and two little boys. One of them is a special needs child."

"I can't help you. Don't you understand that?" She yanked open the door of her pickup and sprang in. Without looking at him, she revved the engine and took off in a squeal of tires and a spray of pebbles.

He watched until her pickup disappeared around a corner. She knew something, but she wouldn't tell. He couldn't force her. If she did tell and Ruiz found out about it, he might kill her. She knew that. She felt obligated to him because he had helped her cross the border and he had given her a place to stay. She seemed nice enough, but she had fallen in with the wrong people. He doubted he could offer her any kind of protection. And now he had lost his chance of finding out what she knew about Eric's disappearance.

Discouraged, he walked back to the cafe with the red umbrellas. The girl who waited tables smiled brightly when she saw him and asked if he'd like another cup of coffee. He doubted she would know anything but pulled out Eric's photo anyway. It wouldn't hurt to ask.

"Have you seen this man before?"

She glanced at the photo. "Sorry. No." Was it his imagination or was she nervous? She turned away to wait on a man and woman who had just sat down at another table. Now her smile was all for them.

Probably she didn't know anything. Or if she did, she didn't want to be involved. He couldn't blame her. Heaving a sigh, he tucked the photo back in his wallet and headed for where his rental car was parked in the next block. Time to start finding some answers.

When Eric disappeared, he had been asking questions of people he suspected were connected to Ruiz's drug trafficking. Eric's wife Terry had told him this. She said that sometimes when he was investigating a case he posed as a buyer. Mark had gotten Sofia Ramirez's name from an FBI agent, who had told him she was Ruiz's girlfriend. Although the agent had passed this information on to Mark, he also warned him not to get involved. As an afterthought he added that if by chance Mark *did* find out anything to let him know. He didn't forbid Mark to look into Eric's disappearance, but he made it clear that if he got in trouble, he shouldn't expect the FBI to bail him out.

Mark decided he would start at businesses along the stretch of highway leading to La Roca and gradually work his way down the coast, but probably the closer he got to La Roca, the riskier it would be. He doubted Eric was alive after all this time. It had been more than a month since Terry had last heard from him. But the family needed closure. Not knowing what had happened to him was tearing them apart. He owed it to her and to Eric to find out what had happened. If their situations were reversed, Eric would have done the same for him.

He had no luck at his first two stops—a shop that sold bait and tackle, and another that took people out into the Gulf to fish. But at the third—the Landing, which rented out boats—he found someone who remembered Eric: the owner, a man named Burkett, who was putting plywood over the glass windows of his business when Mark pulled up in his rental car.

"Yeah, I remember him," said Burkett, a pot-bellied man with a red face and several days' growth of beard. "He asked if he could rent one of my boats. Nice young fella. City type."

"Do you remember when that was?"

Burkett lifted his cap and scratched his head. "A month ago. Maybe more. He owe you money or something?"

"No, nothing like that. I'm trying to find him."

"Oh, are you like a private detective?" He said it jovially, but his blue eyes watched Mark with keen interest.

"No, just a friend."

"Sometimes young fellas like to take some time off. Blow off some steam. Know what I mean?" He winked at Mark.

"His wife asked me to look for him. She's worried."

"Is that so? Why doesn't she just go to the police?"

"She did."

"Then I'm sure it's in good hands."

Mark considered leaving at that point but on second thought decided to see what he could find out about La Roca.

"You know anything about the bar down the road?"

Burkett's smile stayed fixed. He shrugged. "La Roca? What about it?"

"I heard it might be a place where I could pick up a little something special . . . something not on the menu."

The man scowled. "I wouldn't know about that. Why don't you drive down there and ask?"

"Maybe I'll do that."

Burkett reached for another sheet of plywood. "That's quite a shiner you got there."

"I ran into a door."

"I guess so."

"What's with the plywood?"

"Haven't you heard? There's a storm coming. Could be a big one they say."

"Well, it looks like you'll be prepared."

"Can't hurt to be ready. You might just want to think about getting out of town before it comes. They're saying we could take a direct hit."

Was that a veiled threat? he asked himself. Impossible to tell. Maybe just a friendly warning.

"Thanks for the advice. I'll keep that in mind."

For a few more minutes he stood there watching Burkett nail a piece of plywood into place, then walked back to his rental car. When he looked back, Burkett was on his phone. Maybe the call had nothing to do with him. Or then again maybe he had just stirred up a hornet's nest. He supposed he'd find out soon enough.

After he got in his car, he checked his own phone and saw he had a text from Terry. She wanted to know if he had found out anything. He texted her back. *Sorry. Nothing yet.* No reason to get her hopes up just because Burkett had recognized the photo. So far it was just another dead end.

He started his car, but before he could pull away a faded black Buick swerved off the highway and slammed to a stop in front of him, blocking his car. He couldn't back up because there was a low concrete barrier behind him. Two rough-looking men got out, one tall, the other short, and started walking toward him. He told himself to stay calm as they approached, one on either side of the Nissan. They looked Mexican. The man on his side—the tall one—motioned for him to lower his window. He didn't want to, but he decided to pretend nothing was wrong. Maybe he could bluff his way out of it. He doubted they would get violent, not with Burkett nearby.

He smiled as he lowered his window. "You seem to be blocking my way. Mind moving?"

"Maybe you should get out," the tall man said in accented English. He had a black mustache, thick eyebrows, and tattoos on his arms. Intimidating looking.

"Why?"

"Because we can talk easier that way."

Mark pressed the button that locked all the doors. "I think I'd prefer to stay here."

"Nice ride," the man said, looking at his Nissan. "Is she yours?"

He heard the scratch of a key across the front door and then the back. Avis would charge him for that. He reached for his cell phone and dialed 911.

"We asked you so nicely," the man said, pointing a handgun at him. "Some folks got no manners."

This time Mark blasted his horn, hoping Burkett would notice. The man brought the gun even closer to the window. He didn't relish the idea of having his brains blown out. Maybe if he got out he could reason with them. Or stall for time. Surely Burkett had heard his horn and would notice his predicament. And the cops should respond to his 911 call even if he hadn't had time to give them the details. They would hear on his phone what was happening.

He flung his door open, hoping it might knock the gun out of the man's hand, but the man stepped back, keeping his weapon aimed at him. The shorter man stood in front of the car now, looking around nervously to see if anyone was watching.

"So what are you going to do—shoot me right here?" he asked. "Can I at least know why?"

"We're not going to shoot you," the tall man drawled. "We're just going to take you for a little ride."

He didn't like the sound of that. "Where to?"

"You ask too many questions. Now get out of the car."

Mark glanced toward the partially boarded up storefront to see if Burkett had noticed what was happening, but he was nowhere in sight.

These goons might shoot him whether he went with them or not, but it seemed more certain that they would kill him on the spot if he refused. Going with them might buy him some time. Maybe he would think of something. It was possible they just wanted to scare him.

"Do you work for Carlos Ruiz?" he asked once they had all climbed into the black Buick. The car smelled of stale cigarette smoke, and a strip of black electrical tape covered a tear in the upholstery. The tall man with the mustache drove while his short companion with the shifty eyes sat in the back seat with him, the gun pressed against his ribs. He hoped they didn't hit any potholes that might make the gun go off.

"You're awfully nosy," the man who was driving said, glancing at him in the rearview mirror.

"Is this about that girl who works at the bar? Because if it is . . ." He could swear nothing happened if this was about a jealous boyfriend, but his gut told him it was about Eric. Someone had told them he was asking questions. Most likely Burkett. What had he expected? It was a small community. People stuck together.

He thought they might be taking him to La Roca, but they turned off on a rutted dirt lane that led to an old barn. Just far enough off the beaten track that if he shouted, no one would hear him. Too bad he hadn't been more careful how he had gone about his investigation. He had bungled it. And one thing was for sure: he was no good to Terry or anyone else dead.

"How about if I swear to go away?" he suggested when they got out of the car. "We just forget this happened."

"You should've thought of that sooner," the tall man said and spit in the grass.

They shoved him into the barn through the wide open doors and then closed them. It took his eyes a moment to adjust to the dim interior. The only light wafted in from a window in the loft. As his eyes adjusted, he saw the barn was used for storing boats. That was all he had time to notice before they pushed him roughly down on the concrete slab floor and bound his feet and hands with a couple of pieces of rope. He tried to stay calm.

The tall man pulled out his phone and made a call.

"Yeah, we got someone here that Carlos wants to talk to. We're at the barn. Can you send him over?"

Oh, great. He was going to have another run-in with Ruiz. He wondered if he could bargain with him—offer him money. Or silence. Probably not. He suspected Carlos Ruiz was not the sort of man you could bargain with, at least not if he already had a reason to hate your guts. He twisted his hands, testing the ropes. They were tight and it was unlikely he could get out of them before Ruiz arrived. Was this what had happened to Eric? He couldn't help wondering. Had they brought him to this barn, tied him up, and handed him over to Ruiz? And if so, what had happened to him next? Because it was probably going to happen to him too.

"You done this before?" he asked. After all, what did he have to lose? Maybe he would learn something.

"You talk too much," the tall man said.

"Of course, you know if I disappear someone else is going to come looking for me." He thought that might get their attention. He hoped it was true.

"Is that so?" The tall man seemed unimpressed.

"You a cop?" asked the short shifty-eyed man.

"Maybe."

"Then where's your gun? Where's your backup?"

"He hasn't got any backup," the tall man said scornfully.

"A Fed?"

"Shut up, Ramos."

"What if he *is* a Fed?" Ramos was clearly nervous.

"He's no Fed."

"How do you know?"

"Too stupid."

Mark grinned. "Look who's talking."

The tall man kicked him in the ribs. He curled up on his side as the pain shot through him.

"Hey, what are you doing?" Ramos said. "I thought we were going to wait for Carlos."

"He isn't going to make a fuss if this asshole has a few more bruises on him."

"I don't know. I think we should wait."

Mark's mind was working furiously. He was trying to tamp down his fear, but it was rapidly escalating. Would Ruiz be satisfied with just beating him up? What could he say to talk his way out of this?

As he panicked, one of the big doors opened. Their heads turned in unison. The girl stood there silhouetted against the light with that halo of hair around her head like some kind of angel.

He had never been so grateful to see somebody. The sight of her filled him with hope. Surely she wouldn't let them kill him. He wanted to call out to her but stifled the urge. Because, of course, she couldn't save him. She couldn't even save herself.

CHAPTER 4

Sofia peered into the dim interior of the barn, looking for the Anglo. Yes, there he was, lying on his side on the floor, trussed up like a calf at a rodeo. At least he was still alive. Gomez and Ramos stood nearby like two guilty schoolboys on a playground who'd been caught doing something wrong.

"Where's Carlos?" Gomez asked, blinking at the light pouring in.

"He's coming. He'll be here in a minute."

"Why are *you* here?"

She didn't answer. She had known the minute she answered the phone that it was about the Anglo. He had not taken her advice and left. Of course, it was no responsibility of hers if they killed him. It would be his own fault for hanging around when anyone with half a brain would have had the sense to leave. Maybe next time he would think twice about poking his nose into places where it didn't belong.

She didn't want to help him. If she crossed Carlos, she would lose her only chance to get her little boy back. For months she had told herself that. She had put up with so much grief from Carlos just to avoid antagonizing him.

But the memory of the *other* Anglo haunted her. The one Carlos had killed, stabbing him while he was tied to a chair. She knew what Carlos was going to do to the man in front of her as certainly as if he had already done it. Because in a way he *had* already done it. And she had seen him do it. Confessing to Father Angelo had not made her feel any better. She could not forgive herself for having failed to stop him, but what could she have done? If she had interfered, he would probably have killed her too, especially since his men were there watching. So now she had one man's death on her conscience, and unless she did something about it, she would soon have another's.

There was no time to stop and think. After Gomez had called her, she had called Carlos. She had done it reflexively, because he expected her to and she was afraid of what he would do to her later if she didn't. When he didn't answer his phone, she left a message for him. She didn't know how long she had until he got it. Maybe only minutes. If she was going to act, she had to move fast. She grabbed Carlos' handgun from the cupboard drawer where he kept it. No time for anything else. Every second counted.

She didn't stop to lock the door, just jumped into her pickup and took off.

"What's with the gun?" Gomez asked, frowning.

She saw his hand slide toward the gun tucked in his waistband and shot him in the foot. The bang of the gun going off in the silence of the barn was like an explosion, but she didn't flinch. Carlos had taught her how to shoot, aiming at empty beer bottles on fence posts. All that target practice had paid off.

Gomez swore at her and clutched his foot. Ramos backed up, eyes wide with fear, hands held out to show he was unarmed.

"If you reach for your gun, I'll have to shoot again," she told Gomez. "And next time it won't be your foot." She looked at Ramos. "Untie the Anglo. And make it fast."

She knew that at any minute Carlos could pull up in his red pickup. Ramos wasn't going fast enough.

"Cut it with a knife if you have to," she said impatiently.

Ramos pulled out a knife and tried to cut the ropes. Finally they fell away and Mark stumbled to his feet.

"Bitch," Gomez said. "You'll pay for this."

She aimed the gun at him.

"No, don't!" Mark's hands flew up to stop her.

Should she remind him that Gomez and Ramos had been planning to kill him? Or point out that shooting them would gain the two of them some time? No time to argue about it, and maybe he was right. If she shot them, it would mean two more dead men on her conscience, and one was already more than she could handle.

"At least take his gun so he can't shoot us before we get to the pickup," she said.

He eyed Gomez uneasily but took his gun. Gomez gave him a look of pure hatred and muttered something in Spanish.

"Come on. Let's get out of here," he said.

She backed out with the gun still pointed at Gomez and Ramos. Once they were outside, they closed the barn doors behind them and ran to her pickup.

"I'm sure glad to see you," he said as they jumped in.

"Carlos could be here any second. Don't thank me yet."

She gunned it down the dirt lane to the road that led to the highway, keeping her eyes peeled for Carlos' pickup.

"My car's at a boat rental place just a little ways up the highway," Mark said. "The Landing. You can drop me there."

"You have to leave this time," she told him. "If they find you, they'll kill you. And next time I won't be there to stop them."

"What about you?"

"I have to leave too." She had known that when she left the bungalow. There had never been any doubt in her mind. She could not go back and face Carlos after what she had done. This time she had gone too far.

"Where will you go?" he asked.

"I don't know. I'll find somewhere to hide."

"You could come back to Denver with me."

Her eyes remained fixed on the road. Of course she couldn't go to Denver with him. Did he think she would just run off with the first man to come along? Did he think she was that desperate? Was she?

"I don't know anything about you," she said. "What makes you think I'd go anywhere with you?"

"I could help you."

She glanced at him. "Why would you do that?"

"You seem like you could use a little help."

"How do I know you wouldn't turn me in to Immigration?"

"I wouldn't. I swear I wouldn't."

She didn't trust him. She had just gotten herself out of a bad relationship and didn't intend to jump into another relationship with a man she hardly knew. "I'm not going with you."

"Listen. The photo I showed you. My friend. The one who disappeared. You saw him, didn't you?"

That was what he was after. He wanted to know about his missing friend. Yes, she had seen him. She wished to god she had never seen him. She saw him at night in her dreams, pleading for her to help him, and there was nothing she could do.

"You know what happened to him."

Her hands tightened on the steering wheel. He had said his rental car was parked at the Landing. She would drop him there and be rid of him. Then she would figure out what to do next. She couldn't go back to Carlos, not after she had shot Gomez in the foot and helped Mark escape. She was on her own now.

"They killed him, didn't they?"

"What do you think?"

"I have to know. He was my friend."

She glanced at him again. He looked so expectant. "If I tell you, will you let it go? Will you leave and go back to Denver or wherever you came from?"

"What do you know?"

She took a deep breath. "He's dead. He's gone. And if you keep asking questions, you'll be dead too."

"Did Ruiz kill him?"

"Here's the Landing."

She saw his white Nissan—and standing next to it, a police cruiser. Slowing, she debated what to do. She had only seconds to make up her mind.

"It's okay," he said. "I called 911."

Her eyes swept across the parking lot. A red pickup stood near the dock.

"What?" he asked as she shot past the turnoff. "Why didn't you stop?"

"Carlos is there."

"But—"

"Burkett must have called him."

"You think Carlos knows—?"

"About what happened back there? If he doesn't, he soon will. He'll find my message on his phone. Or Gomez will call and tell him I shot him in the foot and helped you escape. Maybe he already has. It's too risky."

"But if the police are there . . ."

She suddenly felt impatient. "Don't you get it? Carlos pays the cops to look the other way."

"So what do we do?"

"I don't know. Let me think."

"You could come back with me to Denver. If you'd testify against him, maybe we could put him away."

"And just maybe they would deport me. Did you think of that? I'm not going to testify against Carlos. Are you crazy? He'd kill me. Even if you locked him away, he'd find a way. I'd never be safe."

Flashing blue lights in the rearview mirror caught her eye and she groaned. The police cruiser from the Landing was in pursuit. That meant the cops knew about what had happened at the barn. There was no other reason for them to chase her.

"What do we do now?" Mark asked.

In answer she floored the accelerator. He braced himself as they swerved around a sharp curve, barely missing an SUV coming toward them. The driver beeped indignantly at them.

"I suppose you know this road really well," he said uneasily.

She didn't answer. So how long would it be before more police cruisers joined the chase? She had spotted only one at the Landing, but soon there would be an APB out on them and any cruiser they saw would be on the lookout for them.

"We'll have to turn around and go south. Maybe we can lose them in Corpus Christi."

"How are we going to get turned around with a police car following us?" he asked.

She smiled. "Just watch."

Turning off at the first marina, she tore through the parking lot at an unsafe speed, managing somehow not to hit any boats, cars, or pedestrians. Then they took off down the highway, the cruiser still in pursuit. It didn't try to stop them, just trailed several car lengths behind as they sped south down the length of Mustang Island. It was still behind them when they crossed onto Padre Island and moments later when the causeway came into view stretching gracefully across the lagoon to Corpus Christi.

"They're still following us," Mark said as they started across the causeway bridge.

"They won't try to stop us on the causeway. It would tie up traffic."

"Sorry I got you involved in this."

She stole a glance at him. She had met him only yesterday, but in that short time he had managed to turn her world upside down. She had been used to the routine of her life, working at the bar, relaxing at the beach, living with Carlos. Now she was on the run from the law *and* Carlos with no idea what to do next. But she did not regret what she had done. For the first time since crossing the border she felt free.

The police cruiser was still tailing them as they came off the causeway.

"Maybe we could outrun them," Mark suggested.

"Not likely," she said. "But maybe we can lose them in traffic."

At the first opportunity she exited the freeway and headed for the nearest business district. She had to slow down as traffic grew thicker. For a while she hit green lights. When the light ahead turned red, she swore under her breath. She could run it, but what if she hit a car? Or a car hit them? She hated to chance it. Her eyes flew to the rearview mirror. The police cruiser was still there. She would have to do something soon if she wanted to lose it.

Seeing a break in traffic, she made a quick right turn. At least they were moving again. They hit two green lights in a row. At the next intersection she took a left on a green arrow. The police cruiser was nowhere in sight. Maybe she had lost it. She saw a parking garage and swung into it. If they were lucky, it would take the police awhile to find them. She drove higher in the structure and found an obscure corner to park in.

"Now what?" Mark asked. "Are we going to steal a car?"

She gave him a look. "Do you know how to steal a car?"

"No."

Evidently he thought she did. Because she was Hispanic and from an impoverished country. She sighed. "Come on. We're not going to just sit here and wait for them to find us."

CHAPTER 5

"What are you doing?" Mark asked, glancing anxiously at the nearby ramp as if he expected to see the police cruiser appear.

She had pulled out her cellphone just as they were about to walk from the parking structure into the adjoining Macy's store.

"Calling a friend."

"*Now?*"

She turned away and cupped her hand around the phone as a woman emerged from Macy's carrying a shopping bag. Within a couple of rings someone picked up. She felt a wave of relief when she heard her friend's voice.

"Jackie? It's Sofia. You said if I ever needed help . . ." The words tumbled out in a rush.

"Good god, did you *leave* him?"

"Sort of."

"I hope that means you did."

She looked around to see if there were any police or security guards nearby. She could hear the traffic from the street. Somewhere a car alarm went off. "Look, I can't explain right now, but I need a favor."

"What sort of favor?"

"I need a place to stay. Just for tonight."

"Not a problem. You can stay at my place."

She hesitated. "I don't have my pickup."

"Got it. You need a ride. So where are you?"

"Downtown. Could you meet me at the Gallery?"

"Sure. I'll be there in fifteen minutes. No, better make that twenty."

Mark was watching her as she slipped her phone back in her purse.

"What was that all about?"

"I have a friend who will help us. But we have to catch a bus to get to the meeting place."

"You trust this friend?"

"Yes."

"Okay, but first let's find you a hat."

"A hat?" She glanced at him in confusion. Why would she need a hat?

He just smiled and pulled open the glass door before them.

To stand there and argue was a waste of precious time, so she stepped through the door he was holding open for her into the air-conditioned interior of the store. They rode down an escalator to the women's department, where he steered her to a rack of hats despite her protests that she didn't need a hat. She was still protesting when he snatched up a broad-brimmed straw hat and placed it on her head.

"Perfect. Don't look up at any security cameras and they won't be able to see your face."

Now she understood. She glimpsed her reflection in a nearby mirror and barely recognized herself. A stranger looked back at her.

"A good thing I brought cash," he said as they walked away. "They won't be able to track us with my credit card. And speaking of tracking, you might want to lose your phone."

She instinctively clutched her purse tighter. "Why? What if I need to use it?"

"You sure you want to take that risk?"

"Do you have yours?"

"It's back in my rental car."

His rental car was in police custody now. "They'll look on it, you know."

He didn't seem perturbed. "They won't be able to see much. It's password protected."

"You don't mind losing your phone?"

He shrugged. "I'll get another one."

It was such an American attitude. Anything could be replaced. Clearly he was not as attached to his phone as she was to hers. She hated the idea of losing hers. It was like losing her purse, maybe worse because she had photos on it and phone numbers. If she lost her purse, she lost just a little bit of cash and a fake driver's license—although she would prefer not to lose the driver's license.

They stopped in menswear next, where Mark picked up two pairs of sunglasses and a baseball cap. When they exited through the glass doors onto the busy street, they were wearing the sunglasses and the hats. She saw their reflection in the display window and thought they looked as if they had stepped out of a spy movie.

"Where to next?" Mark asked, apparently relishing the impromptu disguise. At least it hid his black eye.

"We need to catch a bus." She pointed to one pulling up at the curb at that moment. They ran and managed to catch it before it pulled away.

Mark dropped their fares into the Plexiglas cashbox beside the bus driver, and they made their way up the aisle to a vacant seat. Aside from a few curious glances, no one paid them much attention.

"We're only going a few blocks," Sofia warned as the bus lurched around a corner and they bumped against each other.

She felt awkward sitting so close to him. It was closer than when they were riding in her pickup. Their arms kept accidentally touching.

"If it's only a few blocks, couldn't we have walked?" he asked.

She shook her head. "Not enough time. And this way there's less chance of being spotted."

"I like the hat. It suits you."

She glanced at the cap on his head. "You look like an overgrown boy on his way to a baseball game."

"Hey, it's the best I could do. Besides, I kind of like it."

The bus stopped twice before they reached the corner Sofia wanted. Before she got off, she left her phone on the floor under the seat as Mark had suggested. He was probably right about ditching it, much as she hated to leave it behind. Maybe it would ride around on the bus for a while, and if someone picked it up and took it with them, it might lead their pursuers even farther astray.

Once off the bus, they set off walking at a rapid pace.

"Hurry," she said. "I don't want to be late."

A few minutes later a sprawling modernistic building, part of it topped by odd pyramid-shaped structures, appeared before them with a long walkway cutting through green grass to the entry.

"An art museum?" he said in surprise, seeing the name on the building. "Why are we going to an art museum?"

"Because that's where we're going to meet my friend Jackie."

He gave her a questioning look but pulled out his wallet and paid the entrance fee. They stepped into a quiet air-conditioned corridor lined with paintings. Sofia led the way to the contemporary gallery, where a group of high school students stood about listening to an elderly male docent. Or rather some were listening. Others were looking at their cellphones or whispering to each other. She always felt sorry for the docents, who were volunteers and had to deal with restless students who were often less than appreciative of their efforts.

They sat down on a padded green leather bench in the center of the room that gave a good view of the paintings on all four walls.

"This is where your friend is going to meet us?" Mark asked, looking about.

"Yes. Now just relax. She'll be here soon."

They had removed their sunglasses when they entered the museum but were still wearing the hats. She glanced up at the security camera on the wall, then quickly away again, not wanting to attract attention. She was glad the hat hid her face even if there was little chance museum security would know the police were looking for them.

When the docent finished talking, he herded the students into the next room.

"That's my favorite painting," she said when they were alone. She pointed to a seascape in front of them with green waves curling up into whitecaps, light shining through the waves. "It reminds me of when we went to the ocean when I was a child. My father used to take us to the beach back before it got to be too dangerous."

"My god. Is that you?" He sprang up to take a closer look at the next painting. Against a stormy sky a dark-haired young woman gazed over her shoulder at the viewer. The artist had caught that wary look he had glimpsed so often on Sofia's face.

"My friend Jackie painted that. She's very talented."

"She's the one we're here to meet?"

Sofia nodded. "I come here sometimes to look at the paintings. No one bothers me and I can stay as long as I like. Sometimes I join the tour groups and listen to the docents."

She glanced at the door where the students had disappeared. "This is where I met Jackie. I was standing right there where you're standing, looking at the painting of the ocean, and she asked me if I liked it. I said yes, very much. Then she told me she'd painted it and asked if she could paint me."

She touched the small gold cross at her throat self-consciously and sat a little straighter. "I told her I didn't have time to sit around and let someone paint me, but she pulled out her phone and said all I had to do was let her snap a few pictures. That seemed easy, so I agreed. She painted that from the photographs she took."

"You're giving away my trade secrets," a woman in the doorway said. They turned their heads in her direction. She was in her sixties, a striking silver-haired woman wearing a bright red shirt, black slacks, and leather boots.

Sofia leaped to her feet. "Jackie! Thank you so much for coming. I didn't know who else to call."

"And who might this be?" the woman asked as she came toward them, holding out a hand with a large ruby ring to Mark.

"This is . . ." Sofia hesitated, wondering which of his names she should offer.

"Mark Judd," he said, extending his hand and saving her from having to choose.

"A friend of mine," she added.

Jackie raised an eyebrow.

Sofia glanced at the security camera and lowered her voice. "There isn't time to explain. The police are looking for us. You should know that—in case you don't want to help us."

"Ah, that explains the hat. Of course, I'll help you. How could I turn down my favorite model, whose face got one of my paintings on the wall here? I'm indebted to you. So why are the police looking for you? Did you steal something?"

"No—"

"Did you kill someone?"

This was even worse. "No, but—" Her eyes sought Mark's. "I did shoot someone in the foot."

"Carlos?" Jackie's eyes widened.

"No." Her face felt hot.

"Well, never mind." Jackie waved her hand dismissively. "You can tell me all about it in the car. If you're wanted by the police, we'd better get you back to the apartment."

"Thank you for helping us," Mark said as they headed for the exit.

"Did you shoot someone too?" she asked.

"No, only me," Sofia said quickly. "He didn't do anything."

"I bet you had a good reason," Jackie said, patting her arm.

Sofia glanced uncertainly at Mark. *He* had been the reason she shot Gomez in the foot. For him she had thrown away everything without even giving it much thought. She hoped it had been the right decision.

In the car she poured out the story in more detail as Jackie weaved through busy streets. Jackie was an erratic driver with short bursts of speed and lots of fast braking. Annoyed drivers honked at them and pedestrians glared.

"Well, obviously you can't go back," Jackie said when she had finished her story. "And you can't go to the police."

"If you could help us get out of the city . . ." Mark suggested from the back seat.

Jackie glanced at him in the rearview mirror. "I'm not sure I understand exactly who you are. How is it that you and Sofia know each other?"

"We met on the beach," Sofia said.

"On the beach," Jackie repeated slowly as she sped up for a yellow traffic light. "How romantic. And why did Carlos' men have him tied up?"

"Carlos was jealous. They would have killed him."

"Is that how he got the black eye?"

"No, that was last night when he showed up at La Roca."

Jackie frowned. "Carlos is a dangerous man. I told you that before. You should have left him long ago. So what will you do now?"

"I don't know. I haven't decided."

"I told her she can come back with me to Denver," Mark said.

"With *you*?" Jackie's eyes flicked to the rearview mirror.

"Well, she can't stay here, not now."

"That may be true, but are you her best alternative?"

"He's only trying to help," Sofia said, unsure why she felt the need to defend him. After all, she had asked herself the same question.

"I can give her a place to stay," said Mark. "She'd be safe."

"It's just till I get on my feet," Sofia explained. She didn't know why she said that. She wasn't going to Denver with him.

"Do you have any money?" Jackie asked.

"I'm fine." She had a little cash in her purse, but in any case she did not want to take money from Jackie. She didn't know what she would do for money to survive on her own, but she would figure out something. She had been through hard times before. She could always clean people's houses if it came to that.

Jackie's small apartment resembled a museum storage room with crated canvases leaning against walls and furniture.

Her partner Cat, a tall striking black woman, came striding out of one of the other rooms to greet them. "At last I get to meet you," she told Sofia, smiling broadly and kissing her on the cheek. "Jackie captured you perfectly. It's like you just stepped out of her painting."

"They're on the run from the police," Jackie said.

"Fugitives? How exciting!"

"Are you moving?" Sofia asked, eyeing the crated paintings.

"Haven't you heard there's a hurricane coming?" Jackie exclaimed. "We're getting ready in case we have to evacuate. I don't want to leave my paintings behind."

"Can I help?" Mark asked, looking about.

Jackie's eyes swept around the room. "I suppose you can. An extra pair of strong arms would come in handy. You can help load my car."

"We shouldn't have come," Sofia said. "I didn't realize you were getting ready to leave."

"Nonsense," Jackie said. "What are friends for? If we evacuate, we'll take you with us."

"Are you sure you have room for us?" Sofia asked doubtfully.

"Of course, we do, sweetie." She leaned closer and glanced at Mark. "Him too," she added with a wink.

Cat whispered in her ear.

"Oh, yes, there is one teensy problem. Sleeping arrangements. I'm afraid all we can offer is the couch."

They all looked at the narrow couch with its two purple accent pillows. Clearly it would not hold two people. It would barely hold one.

"It's okay," Mark said. "She can have the couch. I'll sleep on the floor."

"Are you sure?" Sofia said. She suspected the floor would be uncomfortable.

"Unless you'd rather flip for it." He grinned and caught the purple accent pillow she tossed at him.

As they ate pizza later that evening seated around the small oval table that generally served for two, Cat insisted on hearing their story all over again.

"She's a writer," Jackie warned. "Be careful what you tell her or she may put you in one of her novels."

"What kind of novels?" Mark asked.

"Murder mysteries. Her characters get bitten by rattlesnakes, struck by lightning, and fall off cliffs."

"How about hurricanes?"

"Not yet," Cat said. "But that could be coming."

When the meal ended, they turned on the TV to catch the latest news about the approaching storm. Sofia expected to hear about the shooting at the barn, or how she and Mark were wanted by the police, but to her surprise there was no mention of the shooting or of them.

"How could it not be in the news?" she said.

"Maybe Carlos didn't press charges," Jackie suggested.

"It wasn't him I shot. It was one of his men."

"Well, whoever you shot, honey, it didn't even make the local news. It couldn't have been too bad."

"I still think we should be careful," Mark said. "Maybe Ruiz and his men wouldn't have killed me, but it sure seemed like that's what they had in mind."

The news was almost entirely about the coming storm. The mayor had just announced that a mandatory evacuation was now in effect for Corpus Christi and nearby communities. The city was in the path of the storm. High winds and flooding were expected. There would most likely be power outages. The mayor emphasized that everyone needed to take the evacuation order seriously. Buses would be provided for those who had no other way to leave.

"Where will you go?" Sofia asked Jackie and Cat.

"Farther inland. San Antonio maybe," Jackie said without hesitation. "We'll try to get out of range and then hole up in a motel somewhere until it's safe to come back."

"It'll be like a vacation," Cat said, smiling. "A little getaway. It'll be fun."

Sofia doubted it would be fun and was reluctant to impose on the two women. The hurricane was complicating everything. She had thought she would only have to find a place for her and Mark to spend the night and then they could leave Corpus Christi tomorrow—rent a car or take a Greyhound bus.

"Maybe we should go back and get my pickup," she said, glancing at Mark.

"No, it's too risky," he said. "The police could still be looking for us. Carlos' men too."

"There wasn't anything on the news about us."

"You said yourself the police may be watching for your pickup."

"Sweetie, he's right," Jackie said. "It's too risky. You should both come with us."

Maybe so, but she hated to be in the way and she hated to leave her pickup behind if she didn't have to. She had so little in the world that was hers. Of course, technically the pickup wasn't hers. It was Carlos' name on the registration, not hers. If she took it, he could claim she had stolen it. She sighed. Why did it always seem as if the odds were stacked against her?

"You okay?" Mark asked as she spread out a sheet on the couch. His hair was wet. He had just come back from taking a shower. Jackie and Cat had retired to the bedroom and they were alone now.

"Of course. Why wouldn't I be?" Sofia said. The matter of the pickup registration was still on her mind. She wondered if Carlos would think of that.

"You don't regret leaving him, do you?" he asked.

A part of her did but she wasn't about to admit it. "I miss my pickup. And my phone."

He grinned. "Same here. I miss my rental car and my phone. Which reminds me. I should probably call Avis first thing tomorrow and let them know what happened."

"There's a phone in the next room. I'm sure Jackie and Cat wouldn't mind if you used it."

She watched him spread the exercise mat Cat had given him on the floor. It wouldn't offer much cushioning. Well, it was only for one night. If they all ended up at a motel tomorrow, she assumed he would have a bed and a room of his own.

She had decided to sleep in her clothes since otherwise it would seem weird with Mark sleeping just a few feet away. She glanced at him. Evidently he had decided the same. He was wearing the black T-shirt and jeans he had on when she first saw him. Any other clothes he had brought with him had probably been left behind at the Alhambra, which meant he was just as short on clothes as she was.

She nestled down between two sheets on the couch. He snapped off the light and stretched out on the exercise mat. She could see his dark outline as he lay there. No, she did not regret rescuing him from Gomez and Ramos, but now she wouldn't have Carlos to intercede for her with Immigration. Finding Diego would be harder on her own. But she wasn't going to give up. Somehow she would find him and get him back.

CHAPTER 6

The next morning when Mark woke, he glanced over at the couch. It was empty, the bedding folded and neatly stacked. Evidently Sofia was already up. He waited a few minutes, listening, but the apartment was quiet. Jackie and Cat must still be sleeping. He got up, folded his bedding, then did some pushups. He felt a little stiff but had slept well in spite of the hard floor. The events of the previous day must have tired him more than he'd realized.

He was just finishing the pushups when Cat walked in wearing a loose white shirt and black yoga pants.

"You sleep okay?" she asked as she crossed the room to the kitchen. "Want some coffee?"

"Coffee would be great."

"Where's Sofia?"

"In the bathroom I guess."

"Uh-huh. I just came from there."

At that moment Jackie swept in wearing a billowing orange caftan and zoris. "Good morning, everybody."

"You seen Sofia?" Cat asked.

"Maybe she's in the studio. I'll check."

Cat turned to Mark. "She wouldn't have gone out, would she?"

"I don't think so." He thought it unlikely when the police might be on the lookout for them, but then how well did he know her? Maybe she had ducked out for a latte or felt the urge to go for a morning jog around the block.

Jackie came back waving a small piece of paper. "She's gone back."

"*What?*" Mark said.

She held out the piece of paper at arm's length. "Read for yourself."

The message was brief. *I have to go back. Don't follow me.* No explanation. He turned the paper over and saw his name printed on the back in bold letters. She had left the note for him. She didn't want *him* to follow her. Did that mean she had gone back to Ruiz?

"She left it beside the phone in the studio." Jackie was watching him. "She didn't say anything to you about this?"

"No."

"Did she seem upset last night?"

"Not that I noticed."

"You two didn't quarrel?"

Both women looked at him as if this were somehow *his* fault. He was as mystified as they were.

"Why would we quarrel? We barely know each other."

"How was she going to go back?" Cat asked.

He thought a minute. "She probably went back for her pickup. She said she hated to leave it." He shook his head. "I don't get it. Why would she go back to Ruiz after what happened?"

Jackie collapsed on the couch. "Maybe it had something to do with her little boy."

"Her little boy?" Mark looked from one to the other. What were they talking about?

"She didn't tell you about him?"

"No."

"Immigration took him away from her. When they released her, they didn't give him back. She's been trying to get him back ever since."

"What do we do?"

"There's nothing we can do," Cat said. "And there's no time. We have to finish packing and get out of here before the storm hits."

He didn't care about the storm. He was more concerned about Sofia and what Ruiz might do to her if she went back. "We have to help her."

"No way," Cat said. "She knows the risk. She had her choice. Tell him, Jackie."

"He'll kill her," Mark said grimly. It was the truth. Ruiz was a cold-blooded killer and she had crossed him. He wasn't going to take that lightly. And it was *his* fault that she was in this situation. If she hadn't rescued him from Gomez and Ramos, she would still have been safe, more or less—if anyone around Ruiz was safe.

"You don't know that," Cat said.

"He's right," Jackie said. "We have to help."

Cat stared at her. "Are you crazy? What can we possibly do?"

"For starters, we could take Mark back there. How else is he going to go back?"

"But the evacuation order—"

"The storm won't hit for another twenty-four hours. We have time. We'll finish loading up the car, and then we'll see what we can do."

Cat looked about to argue but then threw up her hands in defeat. "All right. We'll do it your way, but I don't like it. Just remember—this was *your* idea."

Mark would have liked to leave at once. No one knew how much of a head start Sofia had. Why on earth had she gone back? Was Jackie right that it was about her kid? Why hadn't she told him she had a kid? And what else hadn't she told him?

He hated to think of her at the mercy of Ruiz or his goons. She had risked a great deal to save his life, and now she needed his help. Whatever her reasons for going back, he had to help her. He didn't like getting Jackie and Cat involved, but he didn't really see any other way of going back to Port Aransas, at least not without losing a lot of time, and if Sofia was in danger, there was no time to waste.

For the next half hour they rode up and down the busy elevator, packing the trunk of Jackie's Toyota as other residents packed their cars and SUV's. In addition to Jackie's paintings, they put in a suitcase crammed with clothes and overnight supplies, and a box of books Cat did not want to leave behind. When they were finished, there was not an extra inch of space in the trunk.

They pulled out of the parking structure ready to head for the freeway and found themselves in gridlocked traffic. Cars honked impatiently and ran red lights. The entire population of Corpus Christi seemed to be in a panic to leave.

"Should we get gassed up?" Cat asked, eyeing the long line of cars at the corner Texaco station. She was behind the wheel with Mark in the passenger seat while Jackie sat in back. Because of Jackie's reputation for being a reckless driver, Cat had insisted on driving.

"Let's try a gas station outside the city," Jackie suggested. "It will take too long if we have to wait in these lines."

Mark agreed, relieved that they were finally on their way. They were headed for La Roca, hoping Sofia had gone there or someone there might know where to find her. It was the only place they could think of to look for her since none of them knew where she lived, just that she lived with Carlos Ruiz.

La Roca didn't look open when they got there. A mud-spattered old Chevy was parked outside, but there was no sign of Sofia's pickup.

Mark reached for the handle of the car door, ready to jump out.

"Now wait. Just wait," Cat said, laying a hand on his arm. "I think *I* should go to the door."

"No, it's not safe," he said. "You don't know what these men are like."

"And they don't know me. Which is a good reason I should go, not you."

"She's got a point," Jackie said. "Let her go up."

He didn't like it. What if Ruiz was there? He thought he should be the one to go up to the door.

"Anyway it looks closed," Cat added. "Maybe they've all left."

She was right. It did look closed. If it was, where else could they search for Sofia? He didn't want to just give up, turn around, and go back after they had come all this way.

Cat flung open her car door and stepped out like a movie star from her limousine, head held high, back straight, dressed all in black. They watched as she walked up to the door and rapped. Nothing happened. She rapped again. After a few moments the door opened. A stooped old man with grizzled hair stood there. Maybe a caretaker or maintenance man. She talked to him and then he pointed up the road.

Cat strode back to the car. "He said she's probably at Carlos' house. Apparently it's just up the road a little ways. He said we can't miss it. There's a date palm in the front yard."

They soon found the house—a small run-down looking bungalow. Sofia's pickup was nowhere in sight here either. Mark had assumed that was how she got back. Now he wondered if she had gotten a ride with someone she knew. Or hitched a ride. The red pickup truck in the driveway would be Ruiz's. So at any rate *he* was home.

Cat pulled off on the gravel shoulder of the road several houses away and turned to Mark. "Now this is what we're going to do. You're going to scrunch down so he doesn't see you, and I'm going to the door."

"No, it's too dangerous," he said, shaking his head.

She fixed him with her big dark eyes. "What's too dangerous is you going up there and knocking on his door. He knows you. He doesn't know me."

"She's right," Jackie said. "It makes sense to let her go up there."

"I don't think Sofia's here," Mark said as Cat pulled into the driveway behind the red pickup.

"Well, we'll find out," she said, opening the car door.

They watched her walk confidently up to the door of the house and knock. A minute later it opened. Mark recognized Ruiz, who was shirtless, and scrunched down, as Cat had directed.

"What's happening?" he asked.

"She's talking to him," Jackie said. "Stay down."

"Well, let me know if anything happens."

"She's actually very good at this sort of thing. Once she talked a state trooper out of giving her a speeding ticket by telling him she would put him in her next novel. She even said she would use his real name if he didn't mind."

"Did he mind?"

"Of course not."

"And she got out of the ticket?"

"She did."

"Are they still just talking?"

"Yes."

"What's taking so long?"

"Have a little patience."

"Maybe he has her tied up in there. He could have hidden her truck somewhere."

"Shh, here she comes. No, don't get up yet."

"Well?" he said when Cat climbed in. He was still scrunched down in the seat.

"Let me get us out of here first," Cat said, starting the engine.

"So what did he say?" Mark demanded, sitting up as soon as they were moving again.

She backed out of the drive and pulled onto the road before she answered. "He says she's not there."

"And you believe him?"

"Yes, I believe him. I told him I owe Sofia money for a painting I made of her. I said it was a royalty."

"A royalty?" Jackie said. "No kidding? For a painting? Did he believe that?"

"He said he didn't know anything about it, and then he asked how much, and when I told him a couple hundred, he said I could just give the money to him."

Jackie snorted.

"I told him I had to give it to her in person. He said she wasn't there and he wasn't certain when she'd be back."

"You think she didn't come back here?" Mark asked.

"I don't know."

"So what do we do now?" Jackie asked.

"Nothing we can do," Cat said. "Wherever she is, she's not here. I'll find somewhere to turn around and we head back to Corpus Christi. I assure you Mustang Island is not where we want to be when a hurricane hits."

Mark didn't want to give up, but what else could they do? He thought of the beach where he had watched Sofia through his binoculars, but it was doubtful she would be there. Maybe she had gone to a friend's. Or maybe she had never intended to come back here. He felt frustrated and disappointed. He just hoped wherever she was, she was safe.

At the next intersection they turned around. As they waited for the light to change, a red pickup sped through the intersection.

"That was him," Mark said. "That was Ruiz."

"Are you sure?" Jackie asked.

"Positive."

Cat narrowed her eyes thoughtfully. "Where's he off to in such a hurry?"

"Well, there's one way to find out," Mark said.

"Jackie?"

"You're driving."

"Then let's do this." She turned right and took off after the red pickup.

"Don't lose him," Mark said.

"I won't, but I also don't want him to notice that we're following him."

They didn't have to follow the red pickup far before it pulled off at a little diner—the Country Kitchen, according to the sign in front. Cat drove past, then circled back. The red pickup was parked in front of the diner next to Sofia's black pickup.

"What do we do now?" Cat asked.

"I think I better go in there alone," Mark said, opening his door. He was not going to let Cat talk him out of it this time.

"No way," Cat said, throwing her door open too.

"We all go," Jackie said.

CHAPTER 7

The night before Sofia had slept restlessly, unable to stop thinking about the events of the day. She had trouble falling asleep, and when she finally did, she dreamed she was back in the barn again, arguing with Gomez and Ramos, trying to persuade them to let the Anglo go. Then she woke up. She could see where Mark lay on the floor sleeping. He was snoring softly. No bad dreams disrupting *his* sleep. She wondered what time it was and then remembered having seen a clock on the desk in the next room, the room Jackie used as a studio. She decided to get up and find out what time it was.

Fortunately, the faint light filtering in through the windows helped her avoid stumbling over crated paintings. She reached the studio without mishap and found the clock sitting on the cluttered desk next to the phone, just as she remembered. Four o'clock. In a few hours they would all wake, eat breakfast, and get ready to leave the city. Before they left she would call Teresa and let her know how to contact her through Jackie. She wondered if Teresa knew she had left Carlos. Probably she did since Sofia hadn't showed up for work yesterday. She doubted Carlos had covered up her absence. He would have been angry when he realized she had left him, and when he was angry, he was not good at hiding it.

Her fingers rested undecided on the smooth surface of the phone. It was too early to call Teresa, and besides if someone heard her talking on the phone, how would she explain what she was doing? *Oh, I couldn't sleep and so I just thought I'd call my friend Teresa and give her Jackie's phone number . . .*

She glanced back at the open door. If she closed it and spoke softly, maybe no one would hear her. As for Teresa, it wouldn't be the first time she had called her in the middle of the night. She stepped to the door and closed it so carefully it made only the faintest click. Then she quickly punched in Teresa's number before she could change her mind.

On the third ring a sleepy voice answered. "This better be good."

"It's me—Sofia. Sorry to wake you. I should have waited."

"What time is it? *Four*? Seriously?

"I'm so sorry."

"I can barely hear you. Where are you?"

"At a friend's house. Never mind where. It's better you don't know. Look, did Carlos tell you what happened?"

"He said you guys had a fight."

"He was going to kill Mark—you know, the Anglo."

"Oh, my god." Teresa sounded awake now. "Are you okay?"

"Yes, I'm fine. Listen, I want to tell you how to reach me in case there's any word about Diego. I don't have my phone anymore."

"What happened to your phone?"

"I lost it. It's not important. But I want to give you a number you can call if you need get hold of me—like if you hear anything about Diego."

"That reminds me. Carlos said he needs to get hold of you. And it was something about Diego."

A chill ran down Sofia's spine and her grip on the phone tightened. "What about him?"

"I don't know. But Carlos said it was important. He said if I hear from you, to let you know."

"Have they found him?" She held her breath. If they had found him, she would have to go back.

"I don't know."

She pressed a fist to her mouth. What if he was sick? Or hurt? Maybe Immigration was finally going to reunite them.

"Are you still there?" Teresa asked.

"Yes. Look, I'm going to come back. But don't tell Carlos."

"You'd better hurry then. We may be leaving first thing in the morning. Because of this hurricane that's coming. You know about that, right? Everyone is supposed to leave. But, of course, some people are staying, like Carlos. He says it'll probably miss us. Manuel thinks we should go."

Manuel was Teresa's boyfriend and the father of her little girl. He worked at a meat packing plant in Corpus Christi.

"I'll come to your place—if that's okay."

"Sure. But like I said, don't wait too long. Manuel wants us to get out while there's still time."

Sofia hung up after the call ended. She knew Carlos could be lying. Maybe there had been no word about Diego. Maybe it was just a ruse to get her to come back. But what if he was telling the truth? She had waited so long for news of Diego. She couldn't walk away now knowing she might be passing up her only chance of getting him back.

Before she left the apartment, she borrowed Mark's baseball cap and left a note for him beside the phone. Then she let herself out as quietly as she could.

The city was still dark, and since there were no buses running at that hour, she would have to walk the twenty or so blocks to the parking structure where she had left her pickup. The baseball cap would help her blend, and she would keep in the shadows of buildings as much as possible. This strategy worked until she came to intersections. Then she had to step out into the open under the streetlights and risk attracting attention.

She kept on the lookout for police cruisers but saw only the occasional truck or car or SUV. She hurried past a homeless man sleeping on a bus stop bench and crossed the street to avoid three young men hanging out in front of a convenience store. She would have felt safer if she had one of the guns she had left in her pickup and just hoped her pickup had not been stolen or towed away. If it had, she didn't know how she was going to get to Teresa.

Stores were closed and dark, including the Macy's next to the parking structure. She paused briefly as she debated whether to take the stairwell or the elevator. In the end she decided the elevator was probably safer. She held her breath as she rode up. The doors opened on a nearly empty parking level. A quick glance showed her pickup was waiting where she had left it. As soon as she climbed in, she checked the glove compartment. The two handguns were still there. She felt a wave of relief and started the engine.

It was still dark when she pulled up in front of Teresa's small wood-frame house on the outskirts of Port Aransas. She didn't want to wake the family up, so she tried to catch a little more sleep while she waited for lights to come on inside. By the time they did, the sky was growing lighter. Manuel answered the door, still looking bleary-eyed with sleep. He didn't seem surprised to see her.

"Hey," he said and turned away, leaving her to let herself in and close the door.

Teresa emerged from the bedroom and wrapped her in a hug. "You came alone? What happened to the hunky Anglo?"

"He's probably still sleeping."

"Lucky him," muttered Manuel as he poured coffee into a mug. "Want some?"

"Yeah, thanks."

"Jacinta is still sleeping," Teresa said, glancing toward the bedroom door. "We should keep our voices down."

"So you guys are leaving?" Sofia asked, accepting a mug of coffee. It felt wonderfully warm in her hands, and she breathed in the steam and coffee aroma rising from it.

Teresa's eyes swept to Manuel's. "Yeah, we're going to my sister's."

"How about you?" Manuel said. "You staying or leaving?"

"Not sure. Leaving, I think. But first I have to find out if there's news about Diego."

"About that—" Teresa said, scowling. "I've been thinking. Maybe you should just phone Carlos. It might not be a good idea to go over there if you guys had a fight."

"I know I can't trust him," Sofia said, "but I have to find out if there's been word about Diego."

"Then use my phone," Teresa urged. "Just don't tell him where you are."

"Mommy."

They all turned. Five-year-old Jacinta stood in the doorway in her pajamas, rubbing her eyes.

"Baby, how come you're up so early?"

"I heard you talking."

Teresa rolled her eyes and pushed her cell phone across the table to Sofia. "Just don't tell him you're here. And don't tell him we may be leaving. He thinks we all should just stay put so we can show up for work the day after the hurricane."

Sofia watched Teresa lead her daughter back into her room. She doubted a phone call would satisfy Carlos. He would insist on talking to her in person. But she punched in his number anyway and listened as his phone rang. He was probably still sleeping. Carlos wasn't an early riser. He usually stayed up late watching TV, then in the morning slept in.

Just as she thought her call would go to voicemail, he picked up. "Yeah, who is it?"

The familiar surly voice made her stomach tighten. This was a bad idea. But it was too late now to change her mind. She took a deep breath. "It's me. Sofia."

Silence. She waited.

"Where are you?" he demanded.

Teresa stood in the doorway signaling with both hands not to give away their location. She didn't want to lose her job, nor did she want Carlos to rush over and bang on their door looking for Sofia.

"It doesn't matter."

"Why'd you run off like that?"

"You know why."

"So Gomez and Ramos got a little carried away. That's no reason to take off." He didn't mention that she had shot Gomez in the foot, so she wouldn't remind him.

"Is it true you've heard something about Diego?" she asked.

"Maybe."

"What?"

"No, I'm not telling you over the phone. If you want to know, you come here."

Just what she had expected him to say.

"I'm not coming to the house," she said calmly.

"Okay, somewhere else then. You tell me. Where do you want to meet?"

She covered the mouthpiece of the phone and looked at Teresa. "He wants to meet somewhere."

"How about the Country Kitchen?" Teresa suggested.

She nodded. There would be other people there having breakfast. Carlos was less likely to make a scene in a place like that. "Okay. The Country Kitchen."

Sofia drove her pickup, while Teresa followed on her motorcycle. The sun was up now. Three cars were parked outside the Country Kitchen when they rode up. Carlos had not arrived yet. She debated whether to take a gun in with her. But, of course, she couldn't just carry it in, and it wouldn't fit in her purse. So the guns would have to stay in her glove compartment.

When she walked in with Teresa, they were greeted by Molly, the owner, a rosy-cheeked plump young woman in an apron standing behind the counter. She always had a smile for everyone and was on a first-name basis with all her regular customers.

As soon as they slid into a booth, she strolled over to take their orders.

"You two are up bright and early this morning. What can I get you ladies?"

"Coffee," Sofia said. "Black. And a fried egg."

"Just coffee for me," Teresa said. "I'm on a diet."

Molly rolled her eyes. "Aren't we all?"

When she walked away, Sofia lifted the corner of the gingham window curtain beside them to get a view of the parking stalls. There were three other customers in the diner: a couple of men who looked like construction workers and a solitary man in a cowboy hat reading a newspaper in a corner booth. Not as many people as she had hoped for, but maybe enough to make Carlos think twice about losing his temper.

"You okay?" Teresa said, nudging her.

"Yeah, just nervous. You sure you want to stay?"

"I'm not leaving you here alone to face Carlos."

"Thanks."

Before her order arrived, Carlos' red pickup pulled into one of the parking stalls. She quickly dropped the curtain back in place. "He's here."

Teresa lifted the edge of the curtain on her side of the booth and peeked out.

"What's he doing?" Sofia asked.

"Nothing. Just looking at your pickup, I guess."

A few moments later the door opened and Carlos stepped in. *Take Me Home, Country Roads* was playing over the sound system. His eyes slid around the room. When he spotted the two young women, he started walking toward them.

"Morning, Carlos," Molly called out from behind the counter. "What can I get for you?"

He hesitated. His eyes shot to her, then back to Sofia and Teresa.

"Coffee, I suppose," he said and resumed walking toward them.

He barely glanced at Teresa, his eyes locked on Sofia. He stopped beside their booth, his hand resting possessively on the back of Sofia's seat. "How about we go outside, babe, and talk about this?"

"There's nothing to discuss. You said you had information about Diego. That's why I'm here."

His head turned as the door opened again. Mark entered, followed by Jackie and Cat. Sofia stared at them, surprised. What were they doing here?

At sight of Mark, Carlos frowned and his jaw stiffened. Sofia could feel the tension radiating from him.

"There you are," Jackie said brightly, heading straight for her. But with Carlos blocking the way, she couldn't slide into the booth beside Sofia, so she had to content herself with standing next to Carlos. They looked an odd pair, Carlos with the scar on his face and tattooed arms; Jackie, shorter, with her neatly coiffed white hair and hot pink shirt.

Carlos noticed Cat then and his scowl deepened.

"This is Carlos," Sofia said, trying to keep her voice even as she began the introductions, as if the situation were completely normal. "He was about to tell me something about my little boy Diego."

They all looked at him expectantly.

That's when she noticed the gun in his hand. It had just appeared out of nowhere. She should have foreseen that. Of course, he had come armed.

"Let's you and me step outside and talk about this," he said again, his eyes boring down on her.

"No," Mark said before she could answer. "She's not going anywhere with you."

The gun, which had been pointed at her, veered toward Mark, who was standing several feet away. Honestly, had he no survival instinct? Carlos wouldn't shoot her, but he would have no qualms about shooting Mark.

"All right. Let's go outside," she said, sliding out of the booth and forcing Carlos to take a step back.

"Hold on there a minute," said Molly from behind the counter. "No one's going anywhere." She was holding a rifle aimed at them. "Carlos, you've got a nerve coming in here with a goddamned gun."

"This isn't any of your business," Carlos said. "This is between me and Sofia."

"It's my place and so it *is* my business. Now put that thing away before I accidentally shoot you. You're scaring my other customers."

Carlos looked around as if noticing for the first time the construction workers and the man in the cowboy hat, all staring back at him.

"Just a little misunderstanding."

"I've known you since high school," Molly said. "And I doubt you're going to shoot all of us. In fact, if anything happens to any of these good people after they leave today, I'll see that what happened here gets posted on Facebook." Her eyes flicked to the security camera on the wall. "Now sit down and have a cup of coffee over here at the bar while your friends decide if they want to stay or leave."

Carlos glared at Mark. "This isn't over," he muttered.

Teresa slid out of the booth. "Come on. Let's get out of here," she said to Sofia.

As Sofia passed Carlos, he caught her arm.

"Did you really hear something about Diego?" she asked.

He let go of her arm and looked away.

"That's what I thought." Anger coursed through her. He had no news about Diego. It had just been a ploy to get her to come back.

"Thank you," Jackie mouthed to Molly as they filed out of the diner.

Once outside Teresa hugged Sofia. "Where will you go?"

"I'm not sure."

"You have my number. Call me." She strapped on her helmet.

Sofia watched her roar away on her motorcycle. She felt a wave of sadness and wondered when they would see each other again.

"You want to come with us?" Jackie asked.

She shook her head. "No, I'm good. But thanks for everything."

She saw Mark preparing to climb into her pickup. "Don't you want to go with them?" she asked, surprised. "I'm sure they wouldn't mind."

"And lose my only witness? No way."

There wasn't time to argue. Carlos might come bursting out of the Country Kitchen at any moment with his gun. They needed to leave.

She hastily hugged Jackie and Cat.

"You'll be in touch?" Jackie asked. "If you need anything—"

"I'll be fine. Now go."

CHAPTER 8

Aren't we going the wrong way?" Mark asked.
"There's something I have to do before I leave."
"What?"

Sofia didn't answer. She figured he would guess when she turned into the parking lot of the old Spanish church, slipping between the open gates and braking to a stop.

"I'll just wait here," he said as she started to get out.

"No, come in with me," she urged. "I want you to meet Father Angelo."

Reluctantly he climbed out of the pickup and walked with her up to the church.

"Look, I don't really feel comfortable in churches," he said when they got to the doors, which were standing open. Beyond them the interior looked dim.

She sighed. "Okay, I'll just be a minute."

As soon as she stepped inside, she spotted Father Angelo near the altar, packing up some of the ritual cups used for mass. She hurried down the aisle to him.

"Father, aren't you leaving?" she asked.

"Sofia," he said, looking up. "What are you doing here?"

"I came to see if you need a ride." She glanced around. Half a dozen people were helping to box up hymnals and candles. She should have realized that she wouldn't be the only one trying to help him.

"It's kind of you to offer," he said, "but there's a bus coming. It should be here soon. Would you like to join us?"

"No, I have my pickup outside."

She looked around at the stained glass windows and inhaled the smell of incense and old varnish. She hoped the old church would survive the coming storm. It had been a place of refuge for her during the past nine months. When she had felt most unhappy and defeated, she had come here and Father Angelo had given her hope again and the strength to go on.

Her eyes traveled to Mark, waiting patiently by the door. She had wanted to introduce him to Father Angelo, but the priest was busy and it would be selfish for her to pull him away from his tasks.

"I see someone is waiting for you," Father Angelo said.

She felt the blood rush to her face. "Yes, I'm giving him a lift."

"Don't worry about me." His eyes crinkled behind his glasses. "Go while you still can. They say time to leave is running out."

"I left Carlos," she blurted out. She wanted him to know because of things she had told him in confession.

"Good. Now go."

She retraced her steps up the aisle, looking back when she reached Mark. Father Angelo was talking to a woman kneeling in the front pew. From this distance he looked small and fragile. Strange that she had never noticed that before. She hoped the bus came soon and took him and the others to safety.

"Are you ready?" Mark asked. He looked so solid standing there beside the door. His black eye was starting to fade. He smiled at her.

She looked back one last time, knowing she might not see all this again if the old church was toppled by the coming storm. Then she turned away. It was time to go.

The streets of Port Aransas were more crowded than she had ever seen them before. There was a sense of urgency in the air, just as there had been in Corpus Christi. Everyone seemed to be trying to leave before the hurricane arrived.

"They need police directing traffic," Mark said.

"In case you forgot, we're trying to avoid the police," she reminded him.

"Lucky for us they're too busy to pay any attention to us."

"I hope you're right. Let's see if we can get on the ferry."

If they could get on the ferry, they could head north without going back through Corpus Christi. However, they soon discovered the ferry had a long line of cars waiting to cross. They would have to wait hours to board. They really had no choice but to turn back to the highway and return to Corpus Christi. This route was busy, but at least traffic was moving right along.

After they crossed the causeway bridge, Sofia decided to go south to find a back road that would take them along the southern edge of the city sprawl and avoid the gridlock, but as they tried to get to the road she had in mind, they were caught up in bumper-to-bumper traffic again.

"I think something's happening up ahead," Mark said, trying to peer around traffic on his side of the street.

"An accident?"

"Maybe. I see police cars. Or it might be a blockade of some sort."

She groaned, not eager to run into any police, who might still be on the lookout for them from yesterday. "I can't turn around," she said, glancing at the vehicles behind them.

"Maybe it'll be okay," Mark said. "We may not be on their radar today."

They inched forward. He turned out to be right about it being a blockade. When they reached it, an officer motioned for her to lower her window. He leaned down. "Unless you live over there, miss, you'll have to turn back." He was an older officer, crease marks around his eyes, a little overweight, sweating in the August heat.

He looked at her more closely. "Aren't you—?" He glanced over his shoulder at several other officers helping turn vehicles around. "Are you aware there's a warrant out for your arrest, miss?"

"What for?"

"Car theft. A pickup truck fitting this description has been reported stolen." He frowned. "You got the registration handy? I need to see your license too."

She glanced at Mark, then back at the officer. "Please. Couldn't you let it go? We're just trying to get away from this hurricane that's coming."

He looked over his shoulder again uncertainly. One of the other officers working the blockade was bent down to an open car window. "I don't know. I shouldn't—" He noticed Mark in the passenger seat. "Who's he?"

"A friend."

"Not one of Carlos Ruiz's boys, is he?"

"No."

He readjusted his hat. "If I let you pass, do you promise not to hang around on those back roads? When the storm hits, we don't know if the dam will hold. There could be flooding."

"We're not planning to stick around. We're headed north. I-37 was too jammed up."

"That's because it's the most direct route out of the city." He took off his hat and smoothed his thinning hair, debating. "I'd have you turn around, but that might attract attention. Oh, hell. Go on. Get out of here before I change my mind."

"Gracias. Thank you so much." She could scarcely believe their luck as he waved them forward. Maybe they would manage to get out of the city after all.

Since most cars were being forced to turn back, the road beyond the blockade was open and she could drive faster, but she had to be alert because it was narrow and at times dipped or curved sharply. Houses were farther apart here. The land stretched away in all directions under an overcast sky. It looked as if it might rain soon, but otherwise there was nothing to suggest that a hurricane was coming.

"How long do you think it will take to get out of the evacuation zone?" Mark asked.

"I don't know. It depends on what kind of time we can make."

They rode for a while in silence, each lost in their own thoughts. Sofia hoped that wherever Diego was, he was safe.

"Why'd you go back to Port Aransas anyway?" Mark asked.

"I had to take care of something."

"Jackie said you probably went back because of your son."

She stared straight ahead, her jaw clenched. She didn't want to talk about Diego. Diego was none of his concern.

"You could have told me. I didn't know you had a kid."

She kept her eyes resolutely on the road.

"Did you think Ruiz was going to help you get him back? Is that why you stayed with him?"

She didn't answer.

"Surely you realize he can't help you."

"You don't know anything about it."

"I know he's involved in half a dozen illegal activities. You can't possibly think you're better off staying with him."

"You don't understand."

"Then tell me."

She gripped the steering wheel, her palms sweaty. It had been a mistake to let him come along. What had she been thinking? As soon as she got him to safety, she would be on her way. She owed him no explanation. She had done what she had to do.

"Is your kid—?"

"*Diego*. His name is Diego."

"Okay. Diego. He's here in the U.S., right?"

She tried to tamp down her anger. "Yes, but I don't know *where*. They took him away from me. I don't know where he is." Tears sprang to her eyes.

The pickup lurched. She fought the steering wheel as they veered off the road and struck a fence post. She sat for a moment in shock, trying to comprehend what had just happened.

"Are you all right?" Mark asked, touching her arm.

She laid her forehead against the steering wheel. Why did they have to have an accident now? Just once couldn't things go right?

"Sofia?" There was concern in his voice.

"I'm okay."

They climbed out to assess the damage. The fence post leaned at an angle. There was a dent in the front of the pickup where they had hit the post, but otherwise her pickup looked unscathed.

"It's not too bad," she said. If the engine would start, maybe they could just back up onto the road and continue on their way.

"Come look at this," he said, squatting by the front tire on his side. "You had a flat."

She circled the pickup and squatted beside him. The tire was flat all right, which explained why she had lost control. So it was not her fault after all. Knowing that made her feel a little better, but it didn't change the fact that they were in trouble.

"We must have run over something sharp," she said.

"I'll put on the spare. Maybe it will get us to a service station."

She looked at the empty road ahead of them and wondered how far they would have to travel until they came to a service station. "It might be a long way before we get to one."

He walked to the back of the pickup and leaned down to look at the spare under the carriage.

"Well, there goes that idea. No spare."

"Are you kidding?" She went back to look for herself. Sure enough. There was an empty space where the spare should have been. She stared at it in disbelief. "Why isn't there a spare?"

"Somebody removed it."

"Who?"

"Probably your good friend Carlos."

She didn't want to believe it. "Why would he do a thing like that?"

He shrugged. "You know him better than I do."

If Carlos had been there, she would have given him a piece of her mind. What had he been thinking? She could have been stranded somewhere in the middle of nowhere. Could have been? She *was* stranded in the middle of nowhere. She closed her eyes, counted to ten, then exhaled slowly—a trick she had learned from Teresa. Feeling calmer, she opened her eyes.

"So what do we do now?"

"I guess we walk—unless you have a better idea?"

"Maybe a car will come along," she said hopefully, looking down the road.

He grinned. "When was the last time you saw one? And the ones we've seen have all been heading in the opposite direction—back to the blockade. Do you really want to go back there?"

No, she didn't. Next time they might not be so lucky. Next time they might end up being booked in the county jail.

He walked to the front of the pickup again and looked closer at the flat tire, running his fingers over it.

"What?" she asked, watching him.

"I'm wondering if it went flat for a reason."

"Of course, it went flat for a reason," she said impatiently. "I ran over a nail or something."

"Did you? Are you so sure about that? Did it occur to you that someone might have slashed your tire or punctured it, maybe just enough for it not to go flat right away?"

She stared at him, shocked to think Carlos might have tampered with one of her tires. "He wouldn't have."

He shrugged. "If you say so."

She remembered how Carlos had strolled into the Country Kitchen looking so smug. Did he do something to her tire before he came in? Was that his backup plan if she refused to leave with him? And when had he removed the spare? How long had she been driving around without it? Had he done that on purpose to strand her or had he removed it for some unfathomable reason of his own and forgotten to put it back? Not that it mattered why he had done it. What mattered was that they were stuck miles from the nearest service station with a hurricane on the way.

"I saw a house a little way back," Mark said. "We could walk back and see if we can use their phone. Maybe we could call road service."

She thought getting road service was unlikely when the city was in such a panic, but it would be better than just waiting there, hoping for someone to come by. "What about the guns?"

"We could just leave them here."

She nodded, although she would have liked to take them along. But they had no way of hiding them, and anyone seeing the guns would not want to help them. This was not Mexico or El Salvador, where everyone understood you had to protect yourself. There were no drug cartels or warring gangs or death squads here to threaten them. Still it was hard to tell herself there was nothing to fear. She had lived in fear for too long to be naive about the dangers that could threaten a woman alone. Of course, she was not alone. She had Mark with her. She was glad now that she had brought him along. With him there she was less vulnerable.

"It looks deserted around here, doesn't it?" he said, looking about. Lots of wide open space surrounded them.

"Maybe everyone's already left."

"Over there's the house I saw." He pointed at a house in the distance. Mostly what they could see of it was the roof.

"What if no one's there?"

"Then we'll try someplace else."

"Where's the next house?"

"Farther up the road, I suppose. Just depends which way you want to go."

"That way," she said, looking toward the house he had pointed out.

CHAPTER 9

To get to the house required some backtracking, and Sofia didn't like to backtrack, even if it was only for a short distance. She silently cursed Carlos. If he hadn't sabotaged her tire, they'd be that much closer to putting Corpus Christi and Port Aransas behind them.

A drop of rain fell on her face. She looked up at the sky, which was becoming more threatening by the minute. "I think it's going to rain."

"Maybe this is the start of that storm," Mark said.

They walked faster now, intent on reaching shelter before the downpour broke. The drops increased until a steady rain was falling by the time they reached the house. They sprinted up the steps of the porch. Sofia felt grateful to be out of the rain. She looked at the huge oak tree in front of the house while Mark rapped on the screen door. There was no sound from within. He rapped again, harder. "Anybody home? We're stranded and need a little help."

When no one responded, Sofia decided the situation called for more aggressive measures. Stepping around him, she pulled open the screen door and tried the doorknob. Locked.

"We should go in," she said.

"What do you mean—*break in?*"

She could hear the disapproval in his voice. "Do you have a better idea?"

He looked around as if trying to come up with an alternative.

"If you want to walk in the rain to the next house," she said, "be my guest."

As for herself, she did not intend to walk to the next house. She would find a way into this one. And so she bounded back down the steps, determined to do just that. The rain was heavier now, and it didn't look as if it would stop any time soon. Mark trailed after her looking unhappy as she started walking around the house. There was a vegetable garden in back with stakes marking off the perimeter and twine stretched around it. She tried the back door, but it too was locked. Nearby stood a garage with an unlocked side door. They opened it and peered inside, half hoping to see a car or truck, but it was empty except for a clutter of stored items.

"Well, I guess that's that," Mark said. "Shall we head back to the front porch?"

But Sofia wasn't ready to give up. Walking to the nearest window, she tried to open it, and when she couldn't, went on to the next and then the one after that. On her third attempt she found a window that was unlocked and started to push it up.

"Wait," he said, laying a hand on her arm. "You don't know what's in there." His face was wet with rain, and he looked so earnest it made her smile.

She doubted anything was in there and was willing to take that risk. She brushed off his hand and pushed the window up until there was enough space to climb in.

"At least let me go first," he argued.

"You won't fit as easy as me," she said. "Here. Help me up."

Reluctantly he cupped his hands to give her a boost. She wriggled through the window arms and head first. When she picked herself up, she was in a bedroom, shadowy in the grey half-light. She turned back to the window.

"Go around to the front door," she told Mark, who was looking up at her, the rain running down his face and plastering his T-shirt to his chest. "I'll let you in."

Soon they were both standing in the living room, looking around them like two lost children in a fairy tale. A sofa faced a TV, an armchair sat nearby with a footstool in front of it, and a large oval braided rug lay on the wood floor in the center of the room. Sofia turned on a floor lamp and its light made the room seem a little warmer.

"You do realize breaking and entering is a crime, don't you?" Mark said, lifting an eyebrow.

"Would you prefer to go back out on the porch?"

He muttered something under his breath that she didn't catch.

"Where are you going?" he asked as she walked away.

"To find some dry clothes."

"Now we're going to steal other people's clothes?"

"Borrow," she called over her shoulder.

She retraced her steps to the bedroom. A light switch on the wall turned on a ceiling light overhead, showing a bed covered by a blue spread with a floral pattern. On the floor by her feet a fringed multi-colored throw rug lay on the hardwood floor. Across the room she caught sight of her reflection in the dresser mirror. She looked wet and bedraggled, her dark hair curling, her wet T-shirt clinging to her. Stepping back into the hall, she pulled a towel from the linen closet and tried to rub her hair with it.

Next she searched the bedroom closet for dry clothes. Half were women's clothes and half were men's. She rifled through shirts, tops, and dresses, and chose a peach-colored shirt. After removing her wet T-shirt and drying off, she slipped on the peach-colored shirt. Finding dry jeans was harder. The woman's clothes were a size or two too large for her. In the end she decided to stick with her own jeans even though they were damp from the rain.

She was about to leave the room when a framed photo on the dresser caught her eye. She walked over to take a closer look. It showed a young couple sitting on the steps of the front porch, a boy about Diego's age standing between them. She felt like someone had punched her in the chest. The laughing little boy could have been Diego. That was the sort of family he should have had—smiling, happy, secure. The sort of family she and Hector should have given him. She looked away, blinking back the tears. It hurt so much to remember everything she had lost.

When she returned to the living room, Mark was standing by a window, looking out at the rain. She handed him the towel.

"There are some shirts in there," she said, nodding over her shoulder. "You should be able to find something dry to put on."

"It doesn't look like it's going to stop," he said. "I think this is definitely that storm."

"At least we're under cover." She touched his arm, and he looked at her. They had been alone together in his motel room and in her pickup, and the night before at Jackie's apartment when she had slept on the couch and he had slept on the floor, but this felt different. She was acutely aware that they were alone together and wasn't sure how she felt about that. Better not to get anything started. She moved away to put some space between them.

"Now where are you off to?" he asked.

"Kitchen. To see if they left us any food."

The kitchen was separated from the living room by a bar. Otherwise, it was one large room. She checked the big stainless steel refrigerator first. A carton of milk, a tub of margarine, salad dressings in the door, lettuce and eggs in the bins, some frozen packages of meat in the freezer section. The people must have left fast. Next she looked in the cupboards and saw canned soups and vegetables. At least food was not going to be a problem. Now if they just had a phone . . .

"Have you seen a phone?" she asked, her eyes darting about the room.

"No."

He was standing on the other side of the bar, watching her. She wondered what was going through his mind. Maybe it was better not to know.

"If we can find a phone, maybe we can call a tow truck or someone to bring a new tire." Now that they were out of the rain, she felt energized again. Maybe they could still get out of the storm zone before the weather turned really bad.

"I doubt we'll find road service with a hurricane on the way."

Hadn't it been his idea to go look for a phone?

"We can try. I'll check the other rooms. Maybe the owners left a cell phone behind or maybe there's a landline somewhere in the house. It can't hurt to look."

She went back to the bedroom to search for a phone. None on the dresser or the nightstand. She opened and closed drawers just in case one was hiding somewhere.

The next room was a small bathroom. Two beige hand towels hung on a towel bar. A few bottles of lotion stood on the counter under the mirror. A pink bar of soap sat beside the sink. No phone here either.

On the threshold of the next room she stopped with a quick intake of breath. This was the boy's room. A pale blue bedspread with red Spiderman figures covered the small bed. A Winnie-the-Pooh bear sat on the pillow. A yellow plastic crate of toys stood against the wall. Diego would have loved a room like this. Instead he had had just a small mattress to sleep on at the foot of their bed. Was it so wrong to want a room like this for him?

"Did you find a phone?" Mark asked as he stepped out of the master bedroom, buttoning up a shirt he had just put on.

"No." She closed the door to the boy's room behind her, instinctively wanting to hide it.

"What's in there?"

"Their kid's room." She avoided his eyes.

"Okay."

Relief swept through her when he didn't insist on looking at it. There wasn't any reason he shouldn't, and yet she felt the urge to keep it to herself. Maybe she didn't want him to guess how much the room unsettled her.

"There's a TV in the living room," he said. "Maybe we can find some updates on the storm."

According to the latest news bulletin on TV, wind speeds had increased to eighty miles per hour, and the storm had been officially upgraded to a hurricane. While it would not make landfall for another twenty-four hours, people who had not already left were now being advised to shelter in place. There was footage of stalled traffic in the rain in downtown Corpus Christi. Gas stations were running out of fuel, and grocery stores were running out of food and batteries. The public was advised to have bottled water on hand and be prepared for power outages.

They were sitting on the sofa in front of the TV eating a belated lunch of tuna and mayo sandwiches while listening to this bulletin.

"I guess that means we're stuck here," Mark said. "Even if we walk to the next house, and even if we find people there, apparently it's too late to get out of the storm zone."

"You should have gone with Jackie and Cat," Sofia said. "I bet they got out."

"It's okay. It's not your fault."

"But the tire—"

"That wasn't your fault either."

Maybe not, but look how much trouble she had caused for him since she met him on the beach. Carlos had given him a black eye. Gomez and Ramos had kidnapped him and tied him up in that barn. Carlos had threatened him with a gun at the

Country Kitchen. And the flat tire had probably been Carlos' handiwork too.

"Where will you go when this is over?" he asked, tucking the last bite of his sandwich in his mouth.

She shrugged. "I don't know. Houston maybe."

"Why Houston?"

"They have an ICE office there."

He looked surprised. "You aren't worried that they might deport you?"

"I'll take that chance. I have to find Diego if I can."

"They should never have taken him away from you."

But they had. What she wouldn't give to turn back the clock to that moment in time when they had pulled him from her arms and carried him off crying. She should never have let them take him. And yet how could she have stopped them?

"I'll bet it was hard, coming all that way from El Salvador with a kid," he said.

"I had no choice. I couldn't leave him behind. And if we'd stayed, we'd be dead."

"Sounds like a rough place to live."

Her eyes moved around the room. So unlike the little apartment she had shared with Hector. If only they had not gone that day to the grocery store. Or they had gone earlier or later. Poor Hector. He had not deserved to die on the pavement like a dog.

"You have no idea what it's like there," she said bitterly. "The gangs, the violence. They killed my parents, my brother, my husband. They would have killed me if I'd stayed. I had no money to buy food, and it wasn't safe to go outside the house. For Diego's sake I had to leave."

It was raining harder now, the rain pounding the roof and pelting the windows. It was as if they were alone in the world, just the two of them. She no longer felt nervous. She trusted him.

"Did you and Diego make the journey alone?" he asked.

"No, there were four of us when we started—me, Diego, Rosa, and Maria. Rosa was only thirteen years old. Just a kid. Maria was a year younger than me. She was running away to avoid being forced to marry a gang member. It wasn't too bad until we got near the border. We were with a bigger group by then. There were these men. They call them coyotes. People pay them to help them make the journey north. But they take advantage and prey on the people they're supposed to help, especially the women and girls. They raped Rosa and Maria."

She fell silent for a moment. "That night they turned on us was the last I saw of Rosa and Maria. I don't know if they made it or not. I got away with Diego, and then we met Carlos and his men. Carlos didn't let his men touch me. I know it was because he wanted me for himself. I'm not stupid. But it could have been so much worse. I was one of the lucky ones."

"What happened to your kid?"

A deep breath. "They took him away from me after we crossed the border. The last time I saw him he was holding his arms out to me and crying 'Mama.'" She put a fist to her mouth. Just talking about it made her want to cry. "A woman who worked for ICE took him away. She said it was standard procedure. I let them take him. I thought they were just putting him in a place for children. But later when I tried to find out where he was, they said they didn't know."

"How could they not know?"

She shook her head, unable to hold back her tears any longer. She tried to wipe them away with her fingers. Mark's arms were suddenly around her, and she was pressed to his chest. She sobbed while he held her and comforted her.

CHAPTER 10

When Mark woke, he could hear the rain drumming on the roof and the wind gusting. He had slept on the sofa in the living room, leaving the bed in the other room to Sofia. It was at least an improvement over the previous night when he had slept on an exercise mat on the floor in Jackie and Cat's apartment. Turning his gaze to the windows, he saw it was still early—a grey dawn with a leaden sky. He padded to the bathroom on bare feet and showered. When he came back, he saw through the open bedroom door that Sofia was just waking up. She stretched, still wearing the peach-colored shirt, her hair a wild tangle of curls.

"Good morning," he said. "How did you sleep?"

"The last thing I remember is laying my head on the pillow. How about you?"

"I remember thinking I probably wouldn't sleep a wink with the wind blowing like that."

"Yeah, me too."

"But I did, so I guess I was beat." He looked away, not wanting her to think he was staring. He should give her some privacy. "I was just about to turn on the TV and see if there's any news on the storm."

He returned to the living room, still barefoot, and stepped in a small puddle on the hardwood floor. As he frowned down at it, wondering where it had come from, a drop of water fell on his arm. He looked up at the ceiling. A leak. A minute later he had a pan under it and was wiping up the puddle with paper towels. Now the dripping water fell into the pan with a steady *plink, plink, plink*. He made a mental note to check the other rooms for leaks.

First though he wanted breakfast. His stomach was growling. He turned on the TV so he could keep one eye on it across the bar as he took stock of their options. In an upper cabinet he found a box of pancake mix, in a lower cabinet a skillet, and in the fridge maple syrup. For this last he silently thanked the owners. While he made pancakes, he learned that wind speeds had increased overnight to 110 miles per hour and they were now facing a Category 2 hurricane. The Port Aransas ferry was closed, and so was the Corpus Christi airport. People were urged to stay off the roads. All emergency services would be shut down until it was safe for them to operate again. The city was hunkered down for the storm.

By the time Sofia joined him, he was heaping pancakes on two plates.

"Wow, you cook," she said, sliding onto a bar stool. She was wearing her black T-shirt with her jeans, her hair pulled back in a ponytail.

"A side benefit of being single. It's that or starve."

She raised an eyebrow. "No girlfriend to do the cooking?"

"I'm in between at the moment."

"So why hasn't someone snatched you up?"

"Someone did, but then she changed her mind. Two days before the wedding."

"She broke up with you? Why?"

"She said I was predictable."

Sofia started to laugh and clapped a hand over her mouth. "Sorry."

"It's okay. I'm over it."

"Two days before the wedding? Wow. That must have hurt."

"Like I said, I'm over it." He had been telling himself this for weeks. He was embarrassed now by how much time he had spent feeling sorry for himself. He wasn't the first guy to be dumped by a woman he thought was the love of his life. You picked up the pieces and got on with it.

"When did this happen?" she asked.

"A couple of months ago."

"Did that have something to do with your decision to come here?"

"No, it had nothing to do with it. I decided to come here because my friend went missing." He pushed a glass of orange juice toward her and a plate of pancakes. She forked a few of them onto his plate.

"So tell me about him."

"Okay. We were roommates at college. Sometimes we double-dated. I was there when he met his wife. Oh, and I'm godfather to his two sons."

"One of whom is a special needs child."

"That would be Adam. He's got autism. Works with a therapist."

"I'm sorry about what happened to your friend."

"Sorry enough to testify against Carlos?"

"You really think anyone would take my word against his? A migrant?"

"Yeah, I do."

She shook her head. "You're wrong. I'm nobody. Less than nobody. I don't belong here."

"Sure you do."

"Lots of people disagree with you. They'd like to send me back to El Salvador. They don't care what it's like there." She sighed. "Look, Carlos is not as bad as you think. He was in the foster care system when he was a kid. Never with one family for very long. One bad break after another. Got into car thefts when he was just thirteen. He did what he had to do to get by. Someone like you wouldn't understand that."

"Why are you so sure I wouldn't understand?"

"Because nothing bad ever happened to you."

He didn't want to argue with her. So Carlos had had some tough breaks. Lots of people did. They didn't all turn out bad. Obviously the two of them didn't see eye to eye on Carlos Ruiz. He was surprised she would want to defend him. Maybe she cared about him more than she let on. After all, she had lived with him for nine months.

"We should get ready for what's coming," he said, abruptly changing the subject.

"You mean the hurricane? How?"

"We should fill some containers with water."

"Okay. That's easy."

"And we should round up any flashlights we can find and candles and matches in case the power goes out."

He glanced back at the TV, where coverage of the hurricane was continuing. A satellite map showed the vivid reds, yellows, and greens of the storm like a mad artist's painting.

As they ate their pancakes, they watched a news anchor in rain gear buffeted by the wind and rain while beyond him waves crashed against a pier. He looked as if he might be blown away if he stayed there much longer.

After breakfast Mark found two more leaks, one at the end of the hall near the back door and another in the corner of the living room, where water had been dripping silently on an upholstered chair. It would probably leave a stain once it dried, but there was nothing they could do about that.

Sofia soon had a number of emergency items lined up on the kitchen counter—a couple of flashlights, several fat candles along with matches, and half a dozen bowls and pans filled with tap water. They had also filled a bucket and the bathtub with water.

At two in the afternoon a news bulletin on TV announced that the hurricane had just been upgraded to a Category 3 and was predicted to reach Cat 4 by midnight. Mark had just finished checking all the windows again to be sure they were closed tight when the power abruptly went out. Without electricity the house seemed plunged into twilight and they were much more aware of how strong the wind was. They could hear it howling around the eaves. Occasionally a gust shook the house and rattled the windows.

They made no move to light the candles or turn on a flashlight since there was still enough light from the windows to see their way about, and they wanted to conserve the candles and batteries as long as possible.

"I found two jackets in case we need them." Sofia dropped a couple of yellow hooded rain jackets on the back of the sofa.

"I doubt we'll be going out any time soon," Mark said, looking out the window at the heavy downpour. The wind was thrashing the large oak tree in the yard. He told himself maybe he should have gone outside earlier to make sure there was nothing that could be picked up by the wind and used as a missile. And he should have checked the garage to see if there was any plywood he could have used to board up windows. It was a shame he hadn't thought of these things sooner. Now it was too late. He just hoped the house could withstand the onslaught of the storm.

Through the rain he could just make out Sofia's black pickup in the distance by the side of the road, where they had abandoned it. He blinked. Through the downpour he thought he saw another car standing beside it. A few more minutes of staring convinced him he was right.

"There's someone out there."

"Really?" Sofia came to stand beside him. She brought her face close to the window and peered out at the rain. "I don't see anyone."

"There's a car beside yours. I'm going out to see if someone needs help. Where are those jackets?"

"I'm going with you."

"There's no need for us both to get soaked. You stay here."

"No, I'm going too."

She was pulling on a jacket. It had a hood, but he doubted it would keep her dry in a downpour like this. Oh well, if she wanted to go out in a hurricane, there wasn't much he could do to stop her. He had a feeling arguing would just make her more determined.

When they were bundled up, he pushed the door open, careful the force of the wind didn't tear it out of his hands. The screen door, which was lighter, flew back against the house with a bang, and he just left it there.

The wind was stronger than he'd thought. He held on to the hood of his rain jacket and put his head down, focusing on the ground as he leaned into the wind. Sofia followed close behind. The lane was a quagmire of mud, water running down it in rivulets. The rain stung his face as he tried to step around puddles. Before long his shoes felt waterlogged.

Walking back to the road took them longer than it had taken the day before to walk from the road to the house because the wind and rain were so strong now. They had almost reached Sofia's pickup when she clutched his elbow. He bent his head near her mouth to catch what she was saying over the howl of the wind.

"Gomez and Ramos!" she shouted in his ear.

CHAPTER 11

As soon as she said their names, he had a sinking feeling she was right. It certainly looked like the black Buick Gomez and Ramos had forced him into at the Landing.

When they reached it, he couldn't see if there was anyone inside. The rain was coming down too hard. So he yanked open the driver's door. The car was empty. He stuck his head in and looked in the back seat to be sure. Then he walked to the back of the car to check the license plate. He couldn't swear it was the same. Too bad he hadn't paid more attention that day. He looked around at the curtain of rain. If it *was* their car, where were they? And why were they here? He doubted it was a coincidence they had turned up.

While he had been checking the car, Sofia had the passenger door of her pickup open and was rummaging in the glove compartment. She pulled out the two guns and handed one to him.

"Is it loaded?" he shouted.

She nodded. "We should go back."

They leaned into the wind again and trudged back down the lane that led to the house. The wind buffeted them and the rain drenched them. When they got back to the house, they were soaked.

"How did they find us?" Sofia asked as they shed the rain jackets and tugged off their shoes.

"You've probably got a tracker on your pickup."

She looked up, startled. "A tracker?"

"Probably underneath. I'd say Carlos doesn't completely trust you."

Frowning, she started to pace. "So where are they now?"

They both glanced uneasily toward the windows. He half expected to see Gomez and Ramos peering in at them.

"Maybe they assumed we walked north," he suggested. "They might not have expected us to backtrack."

"What happens when they don't find us?"

"I don't know. They might come back." He didn't want to frighten her, but they should be prepared.

"Are they nuts?" she said. "There's a hurricane out there."

"As soon as it's over, I think we should get out of here. Especially if they know we're here."

"And how do we do that? My pickup has a flat tire and no spare."

"We'll go on foot then."

Her eyes fell on the two handguns lying on the counter. "At least we have those."

"I'll bet Gomez isn't too happy that you shot him."

"He can't be hurting too bad if he's out in weather like this."

That was true. Maybe it wasn't Gomez and Ramos after all. Or maybe it was just Ramos. Somehow the thought of being stalked by Ramos didn't bother him so much. Ramos had seemed much less of a threat than Gomez. But he shouldn't underestimate either of them. "Even if they don't find us, they know we couldn't have gone far."

She burst into rapid-fire Spanish, then shook her head as if to clear it. "I can't believe Carlos would put a tracker on my pickup. No spare *and* a tracker."

"He wasn't taking any chances."

"He was being a jerk." She sighed. "Well, we'd better put on some dry clothes. At least the people who live here left us lots of clothes."

"And food."

"And food," she agreed.

Her eyes strayed to the windows streaming with rain. "Do you think we could light a candle?" There was a wistful note in her voice. With no electricity the house was steeped in shadows.

He glanced at the windows too. Could someone on the road see a candle from that distance in the rain? Probably not. But if someone was lurking about outside, peeking in windows . . . He stopped himself from pursuing that thought. No reason to be paranoid. Surely even Gomez and Ramos were not stupid enough to be sneaking about in hurricane-force winds. They must have found someplace to hole up until it was over. What would it hurt to light a candle? She looked so hopeful.

"Sure. Go ahead."

The flare of the match lit up her face as she cupped her hand around the candle and coaxed it to light. He watched, fascinated. What was it about her that made her seem so different from other women? She was both vulnerable and strong at the same time. He wanted to touch her, but there was a wariness about her that made him hesitate.

As evening came on and it grew darker, they stayed near the candle, its small circle of light a source of comfort as they listened to the wind tear about the house like a beast trying to find its way in. Sometimes a sudden draft made the candle flutter and threw shadows on the walls.

Without electricity they had to eat a cold meal. They made peanut butter and jelly sandwiches and shared an apple and a chunk of cheese they found in the refrigerator.

"What's it like in El Salvador?" he asked as they ate their makeshift meal perched on bar stools.

She took a sip of water from the glass in front of her, gathering her thoughts. "Most people are poor. Jobs are hard to find and don't pay much, although there are rich people. The rich live in gated communities and hire bodyguards and drive cars with bullet-proof windows. They worry all the time that someone will snatch their kids or their husband or wife and demand a ransom."

He watched her face in the candlelight surrounded by that halo of curls. The ponytail was gone, the band that had held back her hair wrapped around her wrist. He saw why Jackie had wanted to paint her. There was something haunting and elemental about her. She was like a woman poised on the edge of a precipice.

"The schools all have fences around them," she continued. "You hear the gunfights between the gangs and the cops. There are so many shootouts. Sometimes you see them too. I saw the police shoot a man in the street who they were trying to arrest. He had his shirt off and you could see his tattoos. That's how you know which gang they belong to—by their tattoos."

He wanted to put his arms around her, but the onward rush of her words and the memories they stirred in her seemed to throw an invisible barrier around her.

"It's like a war between the gangs and the police that never ends. That's the way it's been ever since I can remember. Sometimes it seems like one side is winning and sometimes like the other. Sometimes they make a truce, but it doesn't last for long. The police can't protect us from the gangs, and there's no one to protect us from the police. We're caught between them. The gangs are always recruiting new members. If they want you and you refuse to join, they kill you, or they kill someone in your family."

"Is that what happened to your husband?"

She shook her head. A look of sadness passed over her face. "We were coming out of the grocery store. Two rival gangs started shooting at each other in the parking lot. Hector got caught in the cross-fire. They were shooting at someone else. I was carrying Diego in my arms. By the time I got to Hector, he wasn't moving. There was blood everywhere."

It made his heart ache to think of her watching her husband die.

"I didn't really have a choice after that. We were just hanging on as it was with the money Hector made as a mechanic. After they killed him, there was no more money."

"Do you miss El Salvador?"

She shrugged. "It was home. It was all I knew. Yeah, I miss it. But not the violence. The violence was awful."

"You think you'll ever go back?"

"Not unless they deport me."

"You do realize the longer you stayed with Ruiz, the more likely you were to get caught up in his illegal activities?"

Her forehead furrowed. "Look, I'm not going back to him. I couldn't now even if I wanted to."

Did she want to? he wondered. Before he could ask, there was a terrific splintering sound, followed by a crash. They both jumped to their feet. He looked around wildly, half expecting to find a wall had given way or part of the roof ripped off.

"What was that?" she asked, her eyes wide with alarm.

They rushed to the nearest window. The wind had uprooted the big oak tree in the yard and it lay on its side, its roots thrust up in the air.

"Have you ever been in a hurricane before?" she asked as they perched on the bar stools again.

"No, can't say that I have. How about you?"

She shook her head. "I can't believe Carlos didn't want to evacuate. Can you imagine what it must be like on Mustang Island now? I bet he didn't think it would be this bad. I just hope Teresa and Manuel got out. Jackie and Cat too."

"Too bad *we* didn't get out." He glanced up at the ceiling, hoping the roof would hold. They could hear the fierce roar of the wind as it whipped around the house. The candle fluttered and almost went out. Whenever they stopped talking, they listened to the wind. It was impossible not to. Every so often flying debris struck one of the windows with a loud crack, but so far miraculously none had broken.

"Maybe we should sit behind the bar in case a window breaks," Mark suggested. The bar would help protect them from flying glass.

"Okay," she agreed.

They took the candle and the flashlights with them as they settled down on the floor behind the bar.

"Why are you smiling?" she asked, poking him with her elbow.

"It reminds me of when I was a kid and a couple of my friends spent the night at our house and we watched scary movies after my parents went to bed."

"Only in this one the zombies are real."

He grinned. "Yes, I guess they are."

"I doubt we're going to be able to sleep tonight."

"If it keeps up like this, you're probably right," he agreed.

"Have you got anyone who's worried about you?" she asked.

"My mom would be if she knew I was here, but I didn't tell her. She thinks I'm at home in Colorado."

Sofia smiled. "Let me guess. Sitting in front of your TV watching the news about the hurricane."

"Probably."

She hugged her knees. "So is your name really Mark Judd?"

"Yes, of course it is. You saw my driver's license."

"Okay. But you're not a software engineer, right?"

"No."

"And not an undercover cop or FBI."

"No."

"What then?"

"You really want to know?"

"Yes."

"I teach high school math."

"No kidding?"

"Are you disappointed?"

"Why would I be disappointed?"

"It's not very exciting."

She propped her chin on her knees. "You risked your life to come down here to find out what happened to your friend."

"I didn't know I was risking my life, but yeah. Somebody had to do it."

"You couldn't have just left it to the police or the FBI?"

"His wife asked me, as a personal favor. I couldn't say no."

"So what will you tell her when you go back?"

"That a drug dealer named Carlos Ruiz killed him and dumped his body in the Gulf. That's what happened, right?"

She looked at the candle flame and didn't answer.

As the night wore on, the hurricane showed no sign of letting up. While it seemed impossible to sleep with the wind raging, they both eventually began to yawn. Sofia fell asleep first, her head against his shoulder. He tried not to move so he wouldn't disturb her. Then he nodded off too, only to jerk awake as he realized he had just bumped the candle with his foot. He quickly set it upright again. No harm done, but a house fire could be just as much a disaster as a hurricane. Maybe they should put the candle out and try to get some sleep.

He nudged Sofia awake. "Want to move to the bedroom? I'm worried about setting fire to the house. And if the roof comes off, it may not matter which room we're in."

"Okay."

He blew out the candle and they used the flashlights to make their way to the bedroom. Sofia curled up in a ball and promptly fell asleep, but he lay there a little longer listening to the wind and the relentless downpour. He wondered if the house would hold up against such powerful gusts. But in spite of his worries, he eventually drifted off to sleep.

When he awoke sometime later, Sofia was shaking his shoulder.

"I think it's over," she said.

He lay listening. The wind had died away. The rain was still falling, but after so much deafening uproar the silence was uncanny. "How long has it been like that?"

"I don't know. I just woke up."

"I don't think it's over."

"But the wind's gone."

"I think it's the eye."

"The what?"

"The eye of the hurricane. It must be passing over us."

"I want to see." She started to get out of bed, then cried out and jerked her legs back.

"What is it?"

"Water. Lots of water."

He grabbed a flashlight off the nightstand beside him and beamed it at the floor. Sure enough, the bed was surrounded by murky-looking water.

"How did it get in?" she asked.

The water was maybe a foot deep. His mind raced. If it was flooded in the bedroom, the whole house must be flooded. He thought of storm surge, which he knew could extend for miles inland. Or maybe the dam had burst or overflowed, as the police officer at the barricade had warned them.

"It came in under the doors."

"What do we do now?" she asked.

"Not much we can do."

"Shouldn't we leave?"

"Where would we go in the middle of the night in the dark?"

"I don't know. Up the road?"

"If we have water in here, it's out there too. We should sit tight and wait for morning when we can see."

"What if it rises?"

"Then we're in trouble."

"Don't tell me you're just going to roll over and go back to sleep?"

"I'm not sure I can sleep."

"Me neither." She scrunched closer and he put his arms around her. He could smell the sweet scent of her hair and it tickled his face. She felt warm and very much alive in his arms. He was glad now that he had not married Wendy. In spite of the dangerous situation they were in, he felt exhilarated. How strange that they had met like this! Not in a million years could he have foreseen it. Nothing could have been farther from his mind when he packed a bag to fly to San Antonio to find out what had happened to Eric. Was it possible they would just go their opposite ways when the hurricane was over and he would never see her again?

"I saw it," she said.

"What?"

"I saw Carlos kill your friend."

He went very still.

"It was at La Roca, after they closed for the night. Two of Carlos' men had tied him to a chair. They called Carlos to come back, and for some reason Carlos insisted I go with him. We'd been home maybe an hour or so. He woke me up and told me to get dressed, we had to go somewhere. He wouldn't tell me what it was about. I don't know why he wanted me to go along. Maybe it was to scare me. When we came in, your friend was gagged. Carlos told them to take the gag off. He looked beat up. He had some blood around his mouth. When they took the gag off, he started begging for his life."

She stopped, and Mark waited for her to go on. He could see it was hard for her to talk about it.

"I should have done something." She started crying.

"It's okay. There was nothing you could do."

She shook her head. "You don't understand. He begged *me* to save him."

"You couldn't do anything."

"Carlos had his knife out. I saw it come down. I think I screamed. It happened so fast."

"You couldn't have stopped him."

"I dream about it. I wake up in a sweat, my heart pounding."

"What did they do with his body? Do you know?"

"They took him out in a boat—"

"Did you see them?"

She nodded. "Carlos made me go along. There were four of us—and the body. I tried not to look. I didn't want to see. They were making jokes. When we were a ways out, they dropped his body over the side. They had tied some weights to it to make it sink. It made a splash when it went over. The water splashed us and they laughed."

"Will you testify?" he asked.

She sighed. "I don't know. I'm sorry."

At that moment the wind began to howl again and the torrential downpour resumed. The eye of the hurricane had passed.

CHAPTER 12

The next morning the worst of the storm seemed to be over.

They waded from room to room, checking out the damage. The furniture was mostly ruined. There was a whiff of something unpleasant in the air, as if mildew or mold was already setting in. Their shoes, which they had left on the floor in the living room, were now floating in a foot of water.

"Oh, no, our shoes!" Sofia said when she saw them.

Mark fished them out of the water. "It doesn't matter. They'll just get wet again when we put them on."

She knew it was true, but the idea of putting on wet shoes did not excite her.

Mark wanted to have breakfast before they left, so they searched the cupboards and found a box of Raisin Bran. They ate it dry since the milk was starting to spoil, along with other food in the refrigerator.

Afterward, he waded to the garage to look for anything that might help them navigate the floodwaters outside. When he returned, he was brandishing two ski poles, a grin on his face.

"What are those for?" she asked, laughing. "It's water, not snow."

"These are our walking sticks."

She rolled her eyes. Fins might be more useful.

While he had been rummaging in the garage, she had found two backpacks in the bedroom closet and started packing them. She put one of the guns in each and then added a flashlight and a thermos of water to his and her purse to hers. Peanut butter and jelly sandwiches sealed in plastic bags went into both backpacks too.

As they prepared to leave, Mark secured a folded piece of paper with a smiley face magnet to the refrigerator door.

"What's that for?" she asked.

"I told them we'll send back the things we borrowed."

"How? You don't know their address."

"I'll figure it out. Or I'll drive back down here."

"I'm surprised you'd ever want to see Corpus Christi again."

"Maybe not during a hurricane." He reached over and helped her slip her arms into the straps of her backpack. "Ready to see what it's like out there?"

"No alligators I hope."

"Don't even think alligators."

They left by the back door, where the ground was higher. The wind had died down, but there was still rain. The rain jackets wouldn't keep them dry for long. As they slogged toward the lane, the water deepened until it reached Sofia's waist. She glanced around uneasily. She didn't really expect to see alligators this far from the coast, but she hoped there were no snakes swimming about. She hated snakes.

The ski poles proved remarkably useful, helping them balance and letting them know if they were about to step off the path into even deeper water. They held hands as they walked and that helped. Once when she slipped, Mark held tight and pulled her back on the path.

"Can you see the lane?" she asked doubtfully, eyeing the flat brown stretch of water ahead as they moved away from the house. There were no markers to indicate where the lane lay. The day before when they had walked down it she had not paid much attention because of the driving rain. Now she regretted her failure to observe the route they took more closely.

"I think we'll be okay if we aim a little to the left of your pickup," Mark said.

She peered through the rain at her pickup in the distance. The black Buick had disappeared.

"Yeah, it's gone," he said. "I noticed earlier when I looked out."

She scanned the area but saw no sign of it. "Where do you think they went?"

He shrugged. "I don't really care so long as they're gone."

She didn't trust Gomez and Ramos. Maybe they had given up and gone back to Port Aransas, and maybe they hadn't. She just hoped they weren't lying in wait farther up the road. At least she and Mark had the handguns in their backpacks if they needed them. The thought comforted her.

She looked around again, taking in their flooded surroundings. It was strange to see water everywhere. They seemed to be the only living creatures in the landscape, as if the storm had swept all other life away. Even the trees, stripped of their leaves, looked half-dead.

"What if everyone around here evacuated?" she asked. "What if we're the only ones left?"

"Then we'll find someplace to take shelter and wait for the first responders. Now that the hurricane is over, they're bound to come."

First responders? She hadn't thought of that. She wondered how soon they might come. Probably not before the water receded. They wouldn't be able to get their vehicles through.

"Look," she said a minute later, pointing in the distance at a house on which a tree had fallen. From the road it was hard to see how bad the damage was.

"We'd better check it out and see if anyone's hurt," he said.

It took them awhile to locate the lane that led back to the house and more time to trudge through the floodwater to reach it. She was starting to sweat from the humidity and exertion and was tempted to take the rain jacket off, but the thought of getting her T-shirt soaked by rain again stopped her.

Up close the fallen tree looked even more frightening. It had smashed the roof of the house as if it were made of cardboard.

"I hope no one was home when that came down," she said.

"Anyone there?" Mark called out as they approached.

No one answered.

They waded around the house, looking in windows, most of which were broken. Inside all was dark. The doors were locked. When they got no response, they decided to move on.

The next two houses had also sustained considerable damage. One had lost its roof altogether, and another was little more than scattered rubble and a foundation beside an SUV lying on its side. It looked like a twister had gone through.

A little farther along Mark pointed out a two-story house with boarded up windows that looked undamaged except for some missing shingles.

"Someone's there," he said.

"How do you know?" She studied the house. To her it looked as abandoned as the other houses they had passed.

"Look at the upstairs window, the one on the right."

Something white dangled from the window.

"What is it?"

"A sheet. It's a signal."

They moved slowly toward it, sounding the water with their ski poles as they walked.

As they came closer, a dog started to bark. Mark grinned at her.

"They're probably flooded downstairs, just like we were back there," he said. "Chances are they're sheltering upstairs."

As if to prove him right, a woman appeared at the window and pushed up the sash. "You're not looters, are you?" she called out to them.

"No," Mark shouted back. "Our pickup broke down and we got caught in the hurricane."

"There's just the two of you?"

"Yeah, just us two."

"You can come up if you'd like. The front door's unlocked, but there's a lot of water down there. Might be easier to use the ladder around the side of the house."

"What do you think?" Mark asked Sofia. "Want to go up?"

"Sure. Why not?"

The prospect of getting out of the rain and the floodwater lifted her spirits. She had a hunch they could roam around for quite a while without finding a good place to take shelter. Besides, it felt good knowing they weren't alone out here.

They found the ladder on the other side of the house, just as the woman had said, and climbed it to a second-floor window. Sofia ducked through first and then moved aside for Mark to follow. They were in a small room decorated with framed watercolors of flowers on the walls, very neat and pretty. A sewing machine stood on a narrow table against one wall, a straight-backed chair in front of it. Several boxes packed with food sat nearby—most likely emergency supplies for the hurricane.

The woman who had invited them up stood in the doorway with a black-and-white Border collie by her side. At sight of them the collie started barking again.

"Hush now, Buster," the woman said. "That's enough."

She was pregnant. That was the first thing Sofia noticed about her—a young woman, mid to late twenties, short blonde hair and a fair complexion, wearing jeans and a ballooning shirt over her stomach that might have been one of her husband's.

"When I saw you coming up the road, I was hoping you might be here to rescue us," she told them. "They said on the radio the National Guard is being deployed to help people."

"Sorry," Mark said. "No, we're not with the National Guard. Our truck broke down up the road and we spent the night at a house nearby. Big oak tree in the front yard. It came down last night in the hurricane."

"That would be the Johnsons. Everyone okay?"

"They evacuated before the storm. It was just us there last night. We left a note."

"I'm sure they'll understand."

"You aren't alone here, are you?" Mark asked, looking around.

She hesitated. "No, my husband is here."

Something about the way she said it sounded unconvincing. She looked away and fiddled with her shirt collar like a guilty schoolgirl. *She's alone*, Sofia thought.

"Do you have cell phone reception?" Mark asked.

"Sorry, no. Just the radio. I expect the cell phone towers are down."

Sofia saw the disappointment on his face. He had really been hoping to call for help. So had she.

"Did you see two men in a black car?" she asked the woman.

"I don't know about a black car, but there were two men around here yesterday. My husband chased them off with his hunting rifle. We thought they might be looters. I didn't like the look of them. They said they were looking for someone, but we figured they were looking for houses to loot."

Sofia and Mark exchanged glances. Gomez and Ramos?

"Friends of yours?" the young woman asked, looking from one to the other.

"No," Sofia said quickly. "You're probably right about them being looters."

"Oh, here I am keeping you dripping. I bet you want to dry off."

"I'm afraid we're getting your floor wet," Mark said, looking down at the hardwood floor.

"It's okay. Don't worry. That little bit of water isn't going to hurt it. You should see the downstairs." She rolled her eyes. "It looks like a lake. We stayed down there last night during the hurricane because my husband thought it would be safer. Then when the water started coming in, we grabbed what we could and brought everything up here."

"I'm surprised you didn't evacuate," Sofia said. "I mean, before the storm."

"Oh, I know it looks bad," the woman said, laying her hand on her swollen abdomen. "I'm fat as a cow. But I'm not due for several weeks yet. My husband wanted me to leave, but I wasn't going to drive myself in this condition. Who knows how far I'd have to go to get out of the hurricane's path? They said Houston could get hit too, which it has. My husband wanted to stay because of his grandmother, who lives a couple of miles north of here. She wouldn't leave, and he felt he had to stay and make sure she was safe."

The dog left her side now and trotted over to sniff them, his tail wagging.

"Oh, it looks as if Buster has decided he likes you folks. By the way, you're welcome to stay here with us if you'd like until the water recedes or rescue arrives. We have plenty of food and water. I stocked up before the hurricane. By the way I'm Amy."

They introduced themselves. After they had petted and fussed over Buster, he ambled back to the woman and sat down.

"So your husband's here?" Mark said.

She shifted her eyes uneasily, looking down at Buster. He looked back at her. "Not at this moment, no, but he'll be back real soon."

"You're here by yourself?"

"Well, no, I have Buster."

Buster's tail thumped at mention of his name.

Sofia saw Mark was making her feel uncomfortable and thought she could pose the question more tactfully. "You said your husband chased away two men yesterday."

"Yes, he did."

"And where is he now?"

The woman's eyes filled with tears. Beside her, Buster lay down on his front paws and looked at them with sad eyes.

"I didn't want him to go."

"Go where?"

"His grandmother's."

"How long has he been gone?" Mark asked.

She swiped away tears. "He left just after the downstairs flooded. He moved these boxes of food up here for me and then he left. He said he'd be back as soon as he could. He wanted to make sure she was okay. We would have brought her over here ahead of time, but she insisted on staying at her place."

Sofia glanced at Mark. Was he thinking what she was thinking? Anything could have happened to someone who ventured out in those dangerous conditions last night—even someone who knew the area well. He could have been struck by flying debris. He could have drowned. A tree could have fallen on him. He might even have been electrocuted by downed power lines.

"The truth is I'm scared. I know it's just nerves, but . . ." She laid a hand on her protruding stomach. "If I just knew he was okay."

"I'm sure he's okay," Mark said.

Sofia knew he was trying to reassure the woman, but he couldn't know her husband was okay. None of them could know that. And she sensed it was more than just her missing husband that had the woman worried. "You're not having labor pains, are you?" she asked.

"I'm sure it's nothing." The woman looked down at her hand on her stomach. "Like I said, the baby isn't due yet for a couple of weeks. But—well, it can't come yet, and that's all there is to it."

"It's probably just nerves," Sofia agreed. She hoped that was true. She wouldn't have wanted to be in the other woman's situation, facing the possibility of childbirth while cut off from help by the hurricane.

"When I saw the two of you coming up the road, I thought there comes help," the woman repeated. "I'd just been wishing someone would turn up and here you are."

Sofia doubted they could be much help if the baby decided to come, but she didn't tell the woman that. Best not to make her any more nervous than she already was.

"Maybe I could go check on your husband," Mark suggested. "If it isn't far—"

The woman leaped at the offer. "Oh, could you? I can draw you a map." She turned and ducked into the room behind her before he could say another word.

Sofia kept her voice low, so the woman wouldn't hear. "She said it was several *miles*. Even if she draws a map, you might not be able to find it."

"I have to try," Mark said. "Her husband could be hurt."

"Or dead."

"You stay with her and I'll see if I can find him."

"No, I'm coming with you." She didn't want to be left alone with a woman who looked as if she might give birth at any minute.

"She needs someone here. What if she goes into labor?"

Exactly. "You heard her. She isn't due yet for several weeks. Besides, I know nothing about delivering a baby."

"But you had one."

"That's not the same."

"It's more experience than I've got."

Why did men think women knew more about childbirth than they did? Did they think women were born with this knowledge? When she had given birth to Diego, she had been concentrating on her labor pains and pushing, not keeping track of what the doctor or nurses did.

Before she could explain this, the pregnant woman was back with a sheet of paper on which she had drawn a straight line and a small square.

"This is our house," she said, pointing at the small square with a pencil. "This is the road you just came up." She pointed at the line.

Laying the paper down on her sewing machine table, she hastily sketched in a dozen or more other houses, added several lines representing streets, and circled the square that was the grandmother's house.

Mark folded the paper and tucked it into his shirt pocket under the yellow rain jacket. "Maybe I should leave the backpack here," he said, starting to slip it off.

"No, you might need it," Sofia said, thinking of the gun she had packed in it. What if he ran across Gomez and Ramos out there? Or looters. A lot could happen between where they were and the grandmother's house. She suspected it was farther than the woman's little map indicated.

"It'll be okay," he said, touching her arm.

He couldn't know that! She remembered how he had looked lying tied up on the floor of the barn. Rising on tiptoe, she flung an arm around his neck, pulled his face down, and kissed him. His lips felt soft and inviting. She wanted to argue with him. Why did he have to go? Why did he feel he had to save everyone? Why couldn't he just *stay* and let the first responders go in search of the woman's husband?

He gave her a grin. "I'll be back. I promise."

But was it a promise he could keep? He seemed to have a knack for getting himself into dicey situations. And this time she wouldn't be along to get him out.

She watched him climb back out the window. When he got to the ground, he turned and waved to her as if he were just headed off to the corner drugstore. She felt a catch in her heart as she watched him slog away, the water up to his hips.

CHAPTER 13

A re you two married?" the woman asked when Sofia turned back from the window.

"No."

"I didn't think so."

She turned her head and looked at the woman. *Amy.* That was her name. "How could you tell?"

"Well, I didn't notice any rings for one thing, and then there was the way you kissed him."

She felt the heat rise to her cheeks. "We're just friends."

"Sure." Amy grinned.

Sofia looked down at the puddle that had formed on the wood floor. "Okay if I take these wet things off?"

"Oh my god yes. Let me get something dry for you to put on."

"And you might want to bring a towel to mop up with," Sofia called after her as she rushed away.

After she had changed into dry clothes and left her own wet clothes hanging in the bathroom to dry, she joined Amy in the master bedroom. Since there were no chairs handy, she sat cross-legged on the queen-sized bed while Amy leaned back against a mound of pillows next to her. From there they could look out on the road, or rather on the muddy floodwaters that covered it. Meanwhile, Buster curled up contentedly in a dog bed near the door. Gradually as they talked, the awkwardness of being strangers melted away.

"Excuse me for asking, but you're Mexican, aren't you?" Amy said after offering Sofia a bottle of water and a power bar, both of which she apparently had a large supply.

"No, I'm from El Salvador." Sofia glanced sideways at Amy, hoping she was not one of those Americans who disapproved of Central American refugees. Public opinion was divided about whether to grant them asylum or send them back to the countries they came from. With relief she saw Amy's face light up.

"El Salvador? You're a migrant?"

"Yes."

"Do you have family here?"

"Just my little boy."

Amy's eyes widened. "A kid? Really? What age?"

"Three. Almost four now."

"So where is he?"

She felt her throat tighten. The question she hated to answer. "I don't know. They . . . took him away from me at the border." It was hard to get the words out. You would think with time it would get easier.

Amy frowned. "But you're going to get him back, right?"

"I don't know. It's been nine months since we got here."

Amy's blue eyes teared up with sympathy. "Oh my god. I can't imagine what that must be like." She placed a hand on her stomach and winced. Was she wondering what it would be like to have a child of her own taken from her by strangers, or was she experiencing labor pains?

"Are you okay?"

"I don't think they're labor pains. Just twinges, you know? I'm sure it's nothing." Her attempt to make light of it didn't reassure Sofia.

Don't let it be labor pains. Distract her. "Do you have a name picked out?"

A faraway look came over Amy's face. Had she even heard? *Labor pains*, Sofia told herself grimly. If she had to deliver a baby, could she? Wouldn't there be things they needed to have ready?

"Do you have any supplies around here . . . just in case the baby comes early?" she asked, glancing about the room, which reminded her of a lemon lollipop with its pale yellow bedspread, yellow curtains, and soft yellow throw rugs.

This time Amy heard. "Like what?"

"Something to wrap a baby in. A piece of sheet or a pillowcase. Or a baby blanket."

"Well . . ." Amy also glanced around the room, as if considering what she might have.

And the baby would have to be washed off. "Washcloths and a towel? Hot water?"

Now she looked alarmed. "How can I heat water? There's no electricity."

"I'm sure a pan of clean water will do then," Sofia said quickly. "You have clean water, right?"

Amy nodded, looking relieved.

"And something to cut the umbilical cord with—a knife or scissors. And some way to sterilize them."

"Like how?" Amy frowned again.

"A bottle of whiskey?"

"Al and I don't drink."

Sofia rubbed her forehead with her index finger, a habit she had when she was stymied. "Rubbing alcohol?" Would that work? Maybe better than nothing. Surely help would come before then. If only she had gone with Mark! She did not want to be responsible for delivering a baby. What if something went wrong?

Amy's face relaxed at the mention of the rubbing alcohol. "Yeah, there's a bottle in the bathroom. I'll get it."

Soon they had rounded up all of the items except for a knife. The knives were downstairs and would require wading through the flooded living room. They could do that later, Sofia told herself. She didn't want to get wet again if she didn't have to, and Amy should not go downstairs and wade through floodwater in her condition.

"Were you scared when you had your baby?" Amy asked when they were again seated on the bed.

"Sure," Sofia said. "Everyone's scared the first time."

"I think I wouldn't be so scared if I could get to a hospital. It's being stuck here that scares me. I never imagined a hurricane would come along and interfere." She gave Sofia a rueful smile. "Look, thanks for staying. I really appreciate it. I was beginning to wonder what I would do if the baby starts to come and Al isn't here."

"Don't mention it." Sofia looked around again at the room with its pale yellow throw rugs and cheerful yellow curtains.

What would it be like to fall asleep at night in a room so pretty and spacious? Never in her life had she slept in a bedroom with so much open space. When she had been growing up, quarters had always been cramped, beds shared.

"This is a nice house," she said. "You're very lucky to have a home like this."

Amy grimaced. "I have a feeling the first floor is going to need a lot of work when this is all over."

Sofia thought of the mold that would start sprouting as soon as the water drained away. Maybe sooner. She was probably right.

"Actually I don't care as long as Al's okay," Amy hastened to add. "That's what really matters."

"Don't worry. Mark will find him." Sofia tried to sound confident. She didn't want to increase Amy's anxiety by telling her she had doubts about whether Mark could take care of himself, let alone rescue Amy's husband.

The afternoon passed slowly. Every hour or so they turned on Amy's battery-powered radio and listened to the latest news about the hurricane. Most of it was about the flooding taking place in Houston, where the National Guard was helping evacuate people from their flooded homes.

From time to time Sofia got up, stretched, and wandered to the windows to look out at the watery landscape. It was like being marooned in a drowned world. She wondered when the rain would stop.

Amy pulled out a pack of cards and for a while they played Go Fish. When they grew bored with that, she pulled out some old magazines for them to look at.

Each time Sofia glanced toward the windows, the sky looked more leaden. She wished Mark would come back. Surely there had been enough time for him to go to the grandmother's house and return. What was keeping him?

"You're worried too, aren't you?" Amy said after Sofia had once more wandered over to the window to look out.

"Maybe I should . . ." She was going to say maybe she should go search for Mark.

A look of panic flashed across Amy's face. "No, please don't leave me here alone." She laid her hand on her swollen stomach. "*Please*," she repeated.

As it grew darker, Sofia decided to brave the floodwaters downstairs. If Amy went into labor during the night, she wanted to have a knife handy. Amy explained where to find the knives in a kitchen drawer and gave her a small LED flashlight. Then Amy and Buster waited at the top of the stairs while she went down.

She hesitated before stepping into the dark water that covered the last few steps. It was clammy as it rose around her calves. She was wearing a pair of Amy's shorts and flip-flops, so getting wet was not as bad as before when she was wearing jeans and athletic shoes. She moved slowly, not wanting to stub a toe or trip on an electric cord or something else she couldn't see. She wished now that she had come down while there was still light slanting in through the windows. It was creepy in the dark with the LED light jumping across the walls and shadows swallowing up so much of the room. *Just get it done and get back upstairs*, she told herself.

She had to cross the living room to get to the kitchen. She tripped once when one of her flip-flops caught the edge of a throw rug. To her right the back of the sofa loomed out of the water like some prehistoric monster. It would have to be thrown out after this was all over, as would the rest of the furniture sitting in water. A large flat screen TV on the far side of the room, still above water level, might be salvageable, but the dining room table and chairs would likely be too water damaged—and, of course, the rugs and carpet were hopelessly ruined.

"You okay down there?" Amy called down.

"Yes, I'm in the kitchen now."

She flashed the beam of light across the counter, cluttered with items laid out in the rush to prepare for the hurricane. Amy had said the knives were in the far right drawer. She made her way to it and pulled it open. There they were, lit up by her flashlight, lying in a jumble of utensils. She had her choice of half a dozen knives of various sizes, ranging from paring knives to a butcher knife and even a meat cleaver. She chose a steak knife. Better a steak knife than scissors. The thought of cutting a newborn's umbilical cord with scissors gave her shivers. In fact, the idea of cutting a newborn's umbilical cord with anything gave her the shivers. She hoped it didn't come to that.

"Got it," she shouted and started to wade back through the murky water.

She was nearly to the stairs when there came a pounding on the front door, not two yards from where she stood. Her heart raced. At the top of the stairs Buster started frantically barking.

Her first thought was that it might be Mark and Amy's husband, but why would they come to the front door? Wouldn't they climb the ladder on the side of the house? Unless one of them was injured. But even then why not just open the door? They knew it was unlocked. She stood frozen, unable to make up her mind what to do.

She could hear Amy trying to get Buster to stop barking, but he kept barking anyway.

Then another thought chilled her to the bone. What if it was Gomez and Ramos? She looked down at the knife in her hand and wished she had chosen the butcher knife instead. A steak knife looked puny, and her gun was upstairs in her backpack. If it was Gomez and Ramos, they would be armed.

"What is it?" Amy said. "What's happening?"

"Someone's at the door."

"Who?"

The pounding came again. There was urgency in it, maybe threat. In any case, she couldn't just ignore it.

Several more strides through the floodwater and she was tugging at the door, bracing herself to face whatever was out there.

CHAPTER 14

Mark had not gone far before he realized that the map Amy had given him would not be as easy to follow as he had thought. Some of the street signs were gone, and if he strayed off the route, he could end up missing the house altogether. But in spite of his concern about losing his way, he felt compelled to knock on the doors of the houses he passed to see if anyone needed help. Apparently the residents in this area had heeded the warning to evacuate. It was weird how deserted the place seemed. It reminded him of a movie on TV he had once seen in which most of the people in a neighborhood mysteriously disappeared, leaving just a few behind wondering what had happened.

He wished Sofia were still with him, but one of them had to stay behind in case Amy went into labor and it made most sense for that to be Sofia. He just hoped there was a good ending to his rescue mission once he reached the grandmother's house because he didn't relish the idea of taking bad news back to Amy.

He was maybe halfway to his destination—assuming he had not already wandered off the route—when he heard a dog howling. It was a mournful sound that aroused his pity for the poor creature, probably left behind when its owner evacuated. He couldn't just ignore it. But if he was going to help the dog, first he had to figure out where it was. He took note of house numbers so he could find his route again afterward.

The dog must have heard him approaching because the lonesome howl gave way to barking as he drew nearer. When he found the house, there was no mistaking it. The dog started barking more excitedly, and when he banged on the door, it went wild.

He waited a couple of minutes to see if anyone came to the door. When no one did, he tried the knob, but of course it was locked. Meanwhile, the dog kept barking. Maybe it had been left behind to deter looters, but he hated to just leave it there, not knowing when the owners would return or when rescuers might arrive. He tried a few windows, as Sofia had done at the other house, but they were all securely locked. He told himself he should just go on. There was no way in to rescue the dog and he was wasting time. He could break a window, but if anyone saw him, they might think he was a looter. Then he asked himself why he was so worried someone would see him break in. There was no one around. And even if there were, he would just explain what he was doing. Who would object to him rescuing a dog?

He resumed his search for an unlocked window. When he got to the back of the house, he discovered the windows there had been broken out by the storm. But climbing in from the back of the house looked more difficult than from the front because the windows were higher. He could see the dog now—a dark brown male retriever. It began to wag its tail when it saw him. Not exactly a ferocious watchdog.

"Hey, pooch," he called. "How are you doing in there?"

He made his way back to the front of the house, where there was a porch. Taking the handgun from his backpack, he used the butt to break a window, then climbed in. So much for his compunction about breaking and entering. Once he was inside, the dog seemed happy to see him. It splashed over to sniff him, tail wagging.

He soon discovered that the dog had no food or clean water because of the floodwater standing in the house. So he poured some water from his thermos in a bowl for the dog, then found a bag of dry dog food and put some into a second bowl and placed both on a chair where the dog could eat and drink without the floodwater interfering.

After that, the dog followed him around the flooded house. Next he had to figure out how he could take it with him. It was too big for him to carry more than a short distance, and he still needed to find out what happened to Amy's husband.

He was about to abandon the idea of taking the dog with him when he noticed a round galvanized tub in a small utility room off the kitchen. Probably it would float, but would the dog be willing to sit in it? He took it out on the porch and tried to persuade the dog to climb in. The dog circled the tub a few times as if they were playing a game and then seemed to understand what he wanted and jumped in.

When he was certain the dog was willing to ride in the tub, they set off, the dog floating in the tub, looking about him with interest as if he did this every day. The fact that it was still raining didn't seem to bother him.

Mark was glad of the companionship but hoped he had done the right thing by rescuing the dog. He hated to think the owners might return and be heartbroken to find their family pet missing. He told himself he would see that the dog got to a pet shelter.

His little detour had taken longer than he'd realized, and now he had to find his way back to the street he had been on when he detoured. He looked for house numbers again. Taking the hand-drawn map from his pocket, he studied it. If only Amy had included more details and landmarks. The directions had seemed so easy when she sketched the map. Surely he ought to have found the grandmother's house by now. Was it possible he had gone past it?

He checked his watch and saw it had stopped running. Maybe not waterproof enough for all this rain and dampness. He pulled the thermos from his backpack and took a swig of water. He would go just a little farther, and if he didn't find the house, he would turn back. If he started back soon, he should be able to get there before dark. Even in normal circumstances he wouldn't want to be stranded outdoors in an unfamiliar neighborhood after dark, but the floodwater made that doubly so. And if it was already dark when he went back, he might miss the house altogether and end up completely lost.

He was about to give up searching for the grandmother's house when he spotted the street sign he was looking for. It was leaning crazily but still standing. Feeling elated, he walked faster, certain that the house he was looking for was nearby.

A few minutes later he found it—an old house with its windows broken out and part of the roof gone.

As soon as the tub touched the porch, the retriever jumped out and shook himself. Mark knocked on the door and the dog barked.

"Anybody in there?" he called.

When no one answered, he tried the door. Locked. Of course it was. The dog looked at him inquisitively, as if to ask what he was going to do now. Going to the nearest window, he used his backpack to break out any remaining jagged pieces of glass that might cut him. He had lost his qualms about breaking into houses.

The dog watched him climb in the window. Once inside, he stopped to look around. The place was a mess. The wind had torn through it, overturning lamps, smashing bric-a-brac, and knocking pictures off walls. There was about a foot of water standing on the floor.

"Anybody here?" he called again.

Was that a faint voice answering him or was his imagination playing tricks on him? He went to the front door and let the dog in. The retriever wagged his tail and walked around in the water, sniffing.

The living room wasn't the only room which had sustained damage. So had the dining room, where a tall grandfather clock lay on its side in water and several chairs had been knocked over, but a glass-fronted china cabinet was still intact.

Again he thought he heard a voice, or maybe a moan.

The dog headed for the next doorway, which led to a hallway. As Mark stepped into it, he noticed a light rain falling and looked up. The second story and roof were gone. He saw straight through to the slate grey sky. A groan drew his attention to a man pinned under a beam next to the stairway with debris scattered around him. He was conscious but water almost covered his face. Another inch or two and he would be in even worse trouble.

Mark knelt next to him, assessing the situation. He had dried blood on his head from a gash and the beam lay across his legs.

"I sure am glad to see you," the man said.

"You must be Al."

"That's right. Do I know you?"

"Your wife sent me."

"Did she? Don't suppose you could move this thing off me? I tried but it's kind of wedged, and I can't seem to move my legs."

Mark looked the beam over carefully, debating how to move it without causing more injury to the man under it. "Think you can get yourself out from under it if I lift it?"

"I can try."

"All right. Are you ready?"

"Ready as I'll ever be."

Mark lifted the beam, and with effort Al dragged himself out from under it. When he was clear of the beam, Mark dropped it again.

"Thanks," Al said, pulling himself into a sitting position. "I appreciate that. I was beginning to think I might be stuck for good under the damn thing."

Now Mark could see him better. He was younger than Mark had thought at first, maybe not much older than himself.

He had a shadow of beard starting to appear and that nasty gash on his temple.

"So Amy sent you, did she? Is she all right?"

"I left someone with her—a woman I met."

"That's good. I know she's worried about the baby coming early. I felt bad about leaving her on her own."

"How about your grandmother? Did she make it?"

Al shook his head. "She was upstairs in her rocker when the roof came off and that beam came down."

"I'm sorry. Want me to go up and take a look?"

"Would you? I think she's gone, but it'd be best to check."

Mark climbed the stairs, the dog at his heels. He could see at a glance that the wind had taken more than just the roof. The upstairs rooms looked as if a tornado had gone through. Rain was falling on whatever remained. There was no sign of the old lady or her rocker.

When he went back downstairs, Al sat leaning against the wall, his face pale. "Is she gone?"

"Afraid so."

Al nodded. "Maybe it's just as well. It would have killed her seeing the house like this."

The dog pushed his nose into Mark's hand, and Mark scratched his ears.

"Nice dog you've got there," Al said. "What's his name?"

"I don't know. He's not mine."

"Left behind, huh?"

"Yeah. I hated to just leave him there."

"I thought I'd be able to get back home by midday."

They both looked up at the gaping hole. It was starting to get dark. Clearly they wouldn't make it back tonight even if he could think of a way to move Al.

"We ought to get you out of this water," Mark said.

"I don't think I can walk," Al said. "I think both my legs may be broken."

"Well, there must be something we can do." Through the doorway Mark saw several straight-backed chairs, some standing, some overturned, in the dining room.

"What's it like out there?" Al asked.

"A lot like in here. Wet."

"That's what I figured."

"How about if we get you into a chair, and I pull it over to that sofa? I don't think it's a good idea for you to sit there in water all night."

"Probably not. All right. I'm game if you are."

After a certain amount of maneuvering accompanied by grunts and groans on Al's part, they succeeded in getting him onto a dining room chair. Then Mark dragged the chair into the living room and helped him move onto the sofa. Afterward he rummaged in the cupboards and found a can of beans that he shared with Al, who had had nothing to eat since the previous day. He decided he would sleep in the antique wing chair with his legs propped on a footstool. Not the most comfortable bed, but he would be out of the water. For the dog he placed a thick towel he found in the bathroom in the galvanized tub and set it on the floor beside him. The dog seemed satisfied with this arrangement.

Al was soon snoring, no doubt exhausted from his ordeal. Mark found falling asleep more difficult. He kept thinking about Sofia. He hoped she wasn't mad at him for leaving her behind. He remembered how she had kissed him before he left. Until that moment he thought he didn't really have a chance with her. Now he was eager to get back and find out if he did.

CHAPTER 15

Sofia stared at the girl who stood on the doorstep looking half drowned. She was young—thirteen or fourteen, skinny, shivering, hugging herself. She reminded her of Maria—the same fear in her eyes, the same desperate pleading look. In her mind she could still see Maria on their trek through Mexico—sweaty, dusty, and scared. And still hear her screams the night the men raped her. She and Rosa had tried to watch out for the younger girl, but in the end they couldn't protect her. They had all known the risks of the journey. Traveling through Mexico, whether alone or with others, was dangerous, especially if you were female.

"I saw your light," the girl said.

Sofia looked behind her at the dark night and the steady rain. Where had she come from? Was she alone? She seemed to have appeared out of nowhere.

"How did you get here?" she asked.

"I walked." The girl looked ready to burst into tears. Her face was wet with rain, her hair matted, her T-shirt plastered to her skinny frame. It was not the time to quiz her. Get her inside where it was dry and ask questions later.

"Come in out of the rain," she said.

"No." The girl shook her head. "There's no time. You have to come."

Sofia wasn't about to plunge out into the rain and dark. "Come inside and tell me about it," she urged, not wanting to turn the girl away.

The girl looked back over her shoulder. "I have to go back."

"Come upstairs. We have water and food." Sofia directed the beam of her flashlight at the stairs behind her so the girl could see them. Maybe she was reluctant to enter a stranger's house. No doubt her parents had warned her to be careful of strangers.

The girl's forehead furrowed. "My mother—" She broke off, as if choking on the rest of what she was going to say.

"What about your mother?"

"There was an accident. She's been hurt. She needs help."

Sofia peered out into the dark. She could see only water. How far had the girl walked?

"Come inside and tell me about it. Then we'll decide what to do."

The girl bit her lip, uncertain. Sofia could see her resolve start to crumble. The girl took a hesitant step across the threshold, looking about her apprehensively.

"Watch your step," Sofia said, shining the light on the stairs where they rose up from the flooded floor.

At the top of the stairs Buster started barking again.

"Who is it?" Amy called down.

The girl froze.

"It's all right," Sofia said. "He doesn't bite."

Amy's worried face looked down at them as they climbed the stairs.

"There's been some sort of accident," Sofia explained. "She's looking for help."

"Hush, Buster," Amy said. She gave the girl a big smile. "And who might you be?"

"Jewel," the girl said, watching the dog. "Jewel Jamison."

"Do you live around here, Jewel?"

The girl shook her head. "Over in South Side."

"How about a towel?" Sofia suggested.

"Oh, sure," said Amy and ducked into the bathroom around the corner. She returned with a towel and handed it to the girl, who began to dry herself off. When Sofia gave the girl a bottle of water, she gulped it as if she had had nothing to drink for a while.

"Are you hungry?" Sofia asked.

The girl looked tempted but shook her head. "There isn't time. I have to go back."

"Back to where?" Amy said.

The girl twisted her hands and fingers, looking distressed. "I told her I'd be back. I told her I'd bring help."

"Told who?"

"My mother." She looked anxiously from Amy to Sofia. "She's hurt."

"Where is she?" Sofia asked gently.

"In our SUV. We went off the bridge."

Amy's eyes met Sofia's. "The bridge is a little ways up the road. With all this rain maybe it washed out. I wouldn't be surprised."

"We couldn't see it," the girl said. "The water was so high, but my mother thought we would be okay."

"How is your mother hurt?" Sofia asked.

The girl frowned slightly, considering this. "I think she hurt her leg. Maybe she broke it." She was twisting her hands again.

"Is she bleeding?"

"I'm not sure. Maybe."

The girl noticed the steak knife in her hand and her eyes grew wide. Not wanting to frighten her, Sofia quickly laid it down on Amy's little desk.

"You can't leave me," Amy said, staring at Sofia.

Sofia felt torn about what to do. She had promised to stay with Amy, but the girl needed her help too. And she reminded her so much of Maria. She should have tried to help Maria the night the men got drunk. At the time she could think only about getting Diego to safety. That had seemed more important than anything else. She couldn't save everybody, so she had made a choice. She had tried to save him.

"At least wait for morning," Amy urged the girl. "You might not be able to find your way back to your mother in the dark."

"No, morning may be too late," Jewel said, shaking her head.

Sofia did not want to go out in the floodwaters in the dark to search for Jewel's mother, but there was no one else to do it. She had turned her back on Maria, but she would not turn her back on the girl if she could help it.

"All right," she said, making up her mind. "I'll go with you."

"You *can't*," Amy protested. "What if the baby comes?"

She tried to reassure Amy. "I'll just go see if I can help her mother, and then I'll come right back. If you feel contractions, take deep breaths and try to stay calm. It'll be okay."

"Easy for you to say," Amy muttered. She pressed the heel of her hand to her forehead, closed her eyes, and sighed. "Sorry. I know I'm being unreasonable."

Sofia reached for a couple of bottles of water and tucked them into her backpack along with several power bars from Amy's stash. Since she didn't want to be roaming about outdoors in the dark in shorts and flip-flops, she changed into her jeans and slipped her damp shoes back on. Last she pulled on the yellow rain jacket and slipped her arms into the straps of her backpack.

Buster was watching her with sad eyes. She patted his head and he wagged his tail.

"I promise I'll be back," she told Amy as they started down the stairs.

When they stepped outside, Sofia shivered. It wasn't cold, but it was pitch black. A heavy cover of clouds obscured the moon. Rain was still falling. They waded through thigh-deep water, walking slowly. She didn't want to lose her footing and fall in the water. Who knew what all was in it? Pesticides. Sewage. Chemicals. *Snakes.* They probably shouldn't even be walking in it.

The beams of their flashlights played on the dark surface of the water. It was so silent, just the soft splash of their legs moving through the water.

"How did you find us?" she asked Jewel.

"I told you. I saw your light."

Sofia glanced back at the house and saw the faint glow of the battery-powered lantern in the upstairs windows. She hoped Amy would be all right until she got back. She felt guilty for having left her alone, but she had to try to help the girl and her injured mother.

"Why were you and your mother out here on the road?" she asked.

"We live over in the South Side area. It was flooded there too. My mother thought the road over here would get us to safety. She said it would lead to the interstate."

"It was just you and your mother?"

"Yes, my parents are divorced. My dad lives in Houston now."

Sofia remembered the police barricade. "Wasn't the road blocked off?"

"Yes, but there wasn't anyone around so my mom thought we could go around it."

"When was this?"

"Last night."

"During the hurricane?"

"Yes."

What had the girl's mother been thinking? Who in their right mind would have ventured out during a Category 4 hurricane? Then it occurred to her that Amy's husband had done the same thing. Despite warnings to shelter in place, how many other people had gone out when the hurricane was at its worst? Didn't they understand they could die in a hurricane like that?

"Yeah, it was really scary," Jewel said. "Things were flying all around, hitting our car. And the streets were flooded. Then we went around the barricade and got on this road, and when we reached the bridge, the water just pushed us sideways,"—she demonstrated with her hand—"and our SUV tipped on its side and water started rushing in."

"You were there all day today in your SUV?"

"I didn't want to leave her alone."

So Jewel had not gone looking for help until dark. Why not look during the day when she could see? Sofia decided not to ask. The girl was probably traumatized by what she had been through. She hadn't been thinking clearly. Imagine staying all day in an SUV that had been swept off the road by floodwater and then being stranded in the dark when night came. Even if she was with her mother. Poor kid. That had to have been an ordeal.

She recalled how thirsty Jewel had been back at the house. Apparently she had gone for quite a while without water. Maybe food too. "Have you had anything to eat today?" she asked.

"Just some M&M's I found in my mom's purse."

Now Sofia wished she had brought along more power bars. Jewel's mother would need them. She wondered how badly the woman was hurt. If she had a broken leg, there wouldn't be any way to get her back to Amy's house, but maybe they could make her more comfortable until help arrived. Surely by tomorrow there would be rescuers.

She watched Jewel forging ahead through the water. She seemed to have no fear of losing her footing. And yet she looked hardly more than a child—slim body, skinny legs, flyaway hair.

"How old are you?"

"Thirteen."

She had been right—the same age as Maria. She wondered if Maria had made it across the border in the end. She hoped so. Rosa too.

But now was not the time to think about them. She had to keep her wits about her. She felt like she was walking in a black and soupy void. This was farther than she had driven in her pickup, and she didn't know the terrain. She just hoped Jewel knew where she was going so they didn't end up lost out here at night. Glancing over her shoulder, she saw the faint light from the window of Amy's bedroom had disappeared. She couldn't even make out the outline of the house now. It had been swallowed up by the dark.

"Is it much farther?"

"Just a little way."

She could tell by the asphalt underfoot that they were on the road, but it would be easy to wander off it in the dark. Eerie how still everything was, just the whisper of falling rain and the gush of rushing water. Rushing water? Were they near the place where the bridge had washed away?

"It's just beyond that tree," Jewel said, shining her flashlight on a mesquite tree still some distance ahead of them. She was plowing ahead, eager to reach her mother.

Sofia turned the beam of her flashlight on the tree. She saw no sign of the SUV—or a bridge.

"We have to go this way," the girl said, waving her flashlight wildly to the left.

Surely they were close to where the bridge had been. A current seemed to be tugging at Sofia's legs like an invisible hand trying to move her forward.

Jewel rushed impetuously down an embankment, oblivious to any danger.

"Wait!" Sofia called, worried that the girl would fall and be swept away by the current.

Then she spotted a flash of white—the SUV tilting precariously below, partially submerged in the water. The beam of Jewel's flashlight bobbed over it as she headed for the passenger door.

Sofia descended more slowly, wary of underwater hazards like rocks and downed branches.

She saw Jewel preparing to slip back into the SUV through the open door.

"Wait," she called again.

"She's sleeping," Jewel called back.

Sofia felt apprehensive as she approached the black hole of the open door. She didn't like the way the SUV was tilted. What if it broke loose and started floating away? When she was close, she aimed her flashlight beyond Jewel at the woman behind the steering wheel. The woman was still buckled in by her seatbelt. Her head hung at an unnatural angle, her eyes two half-open slits. A shiver ran through Sofia. The woman wasn't sleeping. She was dead.

"I think her leg's broken," Jewel said. "Can you help her?"

Sofia reached into the SUV and put her arms around the girl. "Your mother's dead."

Jewel shook her head and tried to push her away. "No, she's sleeping."

Sofia held her until she went limp and began to cry.

"I'm sorry," Sofia said. She wondered if Jewel's mother had died when the SUV went off the bridge. Had she had a heart attack? Had she bumped her head? Whatever had happened, Jewel had stayed with her all day hoping she was just sleeping, not wanting to accept the truth.

"What do we do now?" Jewel asked, sniffling.

"We go back. Do you think you can lead us back to the house?"

Jewel wiped an arm across her nose and nodded.

CHAPTER 16

You should go back," Al said. "Amy will be worried sick."
He was stretched out on the sofa, his head turned toward the window. One hand rested on the dog, which had wandered over for some attention.

"No, I'm not going to leave you alone when you can't walk," Mark said.

He had dressed Al's head wound to the best of his ability—washing off the dried blood and using tape and gauze from the medicine cabinet to patch him up. He suspected Al might need stitches for the gash. He might even have a concussion. Nothing they could do about that. Whether his legs were broken or not, Mark didn't know.

He wondered how long it would be until help arrived. No doubt more densely populated areas of the city were a higher priority for rescue efforts, but Al needed medical attention. He could go look for help, but that would mean leaving Al alone, and there was no guarantee he would find help. So he really had no choice but to stay.

As the morning wore on, from time to time the dog wandered to a window to look out, as if hoping it had stopped raining, and when he saw it hadn't, slunk back looking depressed. When he went to the door, Mark opened it for him. He looked unhappy about going out and was soon back. Mark didn't blame him. Unpleasant as it was to deal with a flooded house, outdoors was worse.

There wasn't much to do to pass the time except talk. Gradually he learned a few things about Al, like the fact that he was an attorney specializing in corporate law and how he had met Amy when she came to work as a clerk for his law firm. They had been married for two years and it seemed like the right time to start a family, Al explained.

In turn, Mark told Al he had come to Port Aransas to see what he could find out about the disappearance of his friend Eric, who worked for the DEA and had been missing for more than a month.

"He was investigating a man named Carlos Ruiz, a small-time smuggler and drug-dealer," Mark said. "Ever heard of him?"

"Sorry, no," Al said. "Can't say that I have. So did you find out anything?"

"Enough to be pretty sure he's dead."

"Foul play?"

He nodded. "I found a witness, but she doesn't want to testify. She's from El Salvador and testifying might mean she'd be deported."

"So you've got no witness."

"Yeah. I mean, I understand why she doesn't want to do it. Her kid was taken away from her at the border. She doesn't know where he is now."

Al nodded. "New policy. Separating parents and kids. It's meant to be a deterrent. Instead it's creating a nightmare—both for the parents and for the government agencies that have to enforce it."

Mark leaned forward. "I'd like to help her."

"There's probably not much you can do."

Around mid-morning the dog started barking and ran to the window. Mark went to see what the excitement was. He could hardly believe his eyes. A bearded man in a rain poncho was paddling a kayak down the street. In a few long strides Mark reached the door and flung it open. The dog bounded out onto the porch still barking. At the noise the kayak swung about and glided toward them.

"You folks need help?" the bearded man called.

"Sure do," Mark said, heartened to see another human being out and about.

"How many of you are there?"

"Two—plus the dog." He looked down at the retriever wagging its tail.

"Have you called for help?" the man asked.

"No cell service."

"I can call it in for you if you'd like."

"Thanks. I'd appreciate that. How long until we can get picked up?"

"Might be a couple of hours. Maybe more."

Mark felt overwhelming relief. Their ordeal would soon be over. He'd be able to go back to Sofia, and Al could get medical help.

"One of us is injured."

"How bad?"

"He thinks his legs may be broken."

"I can try to get a helicopter out here."

"That would be great."

He watched the man in the kayak paddle away and then went back inside feeling lighter to let Al know that help would soon be on its way.

The helicopter arrived around noon. They heard the sound of the motor grow louder until it was almost deafening. The dog barked wildly as Mark watched the helicopter land in the middle of the flooded street. Two men wearing rain gear jumped out. In short order they tromped inside and talked to Al and examined his legs. Maybe bruised not broken, they said, but the head wound ought to be looked at by a doctor. Five minutes later they lifted him onto a portable stretcher and hustled him out the door and onto the helicopter.

"You can come too," one said to Mark. "But not the dog. Sorry. Regulations. We can notify someone to pick it up if you'd like."

Mark looked at the retriever, which had calmed down now and was looking back at him. He didn't want to leave the dog behind. He felt responsible for it since he'd been the one to rescue it. But he was also eager to get back to Amy and Sofia.

"I think I'll pass. But send someone for the dog. I'd appreciate that."

"Sure thing."

"By the way, Al's wife, who's pregnant, needs rescuing a couple of miles west of here. Any chance you could pick her up?"

"We'll call it in," one of the men said. "Can't promise though. We're spread awfully thin."

Mark thanked them and watched them lift off.

With Al gone, the house seemed empty. He didn't know what to do with himself. He decided if no one came soon for the dog, he might as well start back. He could take the dog with him if he had to.

He opened a can of beans for lunch, and when he had finished it off he fed the dog and then got ready to leave. He was about to head out the door when he heard the rumble of a motor approaching. The dog barked and began to run around excitedly as if he knew it was coming for him. They went out on the porch to wait for it. The boat was an inflatable with a small motor attached. It had already picked up a family with two small children, all huddled in the bow wearing orange life jackets.

"Are you going over farther west?" Mark asked the man operating the motor, hoping he might be able to get a ride back to Al and Amy's house.

"No, we're headed back now," the man said. "You're our last pick up."

"Could you take just the dog?"

The man scratched his cheek. "You want to stay here? Why?"

"I have to go check on a couple of women who are stranded."

He shrugged. "Suit yourself. You got a leash for your dog?"

"Sorry, no. He's not my dog. I rescued him from a house not far from here."

"C'mon, boy," the man said.

The retriever looked from Mark to the boat.

"Go on," he urged. "Get in."

The dog hesitated a moment longer, then hopped in and sat down in the bottom of the boat and looked back at him with reproachful eyes.

He watched them move away, knowing he would miss the dog.

CHAPTER 17

According to Amy's radio, people were being rescued in Houston and Corpus Christi as well as up and down the coast in smaller communities. Many were posting their plights on social media to let rescuers know where they were. National Guard troops were helping with the rescue efforts. Sofia wished help would come. If Amy and Jewel were rescued, she would be free to go search for Mark. It was driving her nuts not knowing what had happened to him.

Jewel was playing with Buster, rolling a rubber ball across the floor, which he would bring back to her. At least he helped keep her mind off her mother. Poor kid. Every so often she would go to the window, look out, and sigh. They couldn't see her mother's SUV from the house, but that was the direction in which she looked.

"When do you think they'll come?" Jewel asked, turning back from the window. She meant first responders.

"Hopefully before the baby comes," Amy said, her hand resting on her belly. She was curled up on the bed, having contractions. Every so often she would announce, "That was a big one," or "Just had another."

Sofia knew women sometimes had false labor pains ahead of time, and she hoped that was what Amy was experiencing. For a woman who had given birth, she had remarkably little knowledge about the process. All she remembered was that Diego's birth had been easy, her labor short. That and his little red face when they placed him in her arms and his tiny fingers wrapped around one of hers. She had thought him the most beautiful baby in the world. And later as he grew and changed she had been amazed at how much she loved him. God, how she missed him! It was like a piece of her had been ripped away.

"What's that?" Jewel asked, lifting her head, suddenly alert.

Sofia listened. A rumbling sound was coming closer. A helicopter?

"Oh my god," Amy said, sitting up on the bed and looking toward the window. "I can't believe it! Is it the first responders?"

"It's a helicopter," Jewel said, now at the window. "But will they know we're here?"

Sofia sprang off the bed, where she had been sitting cross-legged, idly trying to solve a Rubik's Cube. She ran down the stairs, with Jewel and Buster on her heels. They splashed through the water at the foot of the stairs, threw open the door, and burst out onto the porch. Jewel leaped off the porch and into the water, which came up to her thighs. Sofia followed, not caring if her clothes got wet. They spotted the helicopter in the grey sky as it puttered toward them.

"Here!" Jewel waved her arms and whooped.

Sofia joined in, even though she knew no one in the helicopter could hear them.

As they shouted and waved frantically, the helicopter passed overhead and kept going. They watched in disappointment as it grew smaller until it was just a speck in the sky.

"They didn't see us," Jewel said, staring at the spot where the helicopter had disappeared. She looked on the verge of tears.

Sofia knew how she felt. They had waited so long for rescue and then the helicopter had just passed them by. She should have thought to bring down a white shirt to wave. Maybe they could have gotten the pilot's attention.

"Do you think they'll come back?" Jewel asked.

"Of course, they'll come back." Sofia put an arm around the girl's narrow shoulders. She didn't want her to get discouraged. "I have an idea. Let's see if Amy has some old sheets we can use to get their attention when they come back."

Amy wanted to be rescued as badly as any of them, and so when they asked about sheets, she hoisted herself up off the bed with a low moan and shuffled over to the closet to find some. Over the next thirty minutes Sofia and Jewel used the stepladder to climb on the roof and arrange the sheets to spell out SOS.

Jewel was all smiles when they came back down. "They're sure to see us now," she told Amy.

"That's great, honey," Amy said. She placed her hand on her stomach and frowned.

"Another contraction?" Sofia asked.

"I don't feel so good. I think maybe the baby's coming."

"No, no, no," Sofia said. "You've got to hang on just a little longer."

"Sorry. I don't think I can." She tugged off her jeans and eased herself back on a mound of pillows.

Sofia studied her. Was she really about to give birth?

"Okay, let me see," she said briskly.

The baby indeed was coming. She could see the crown of its head between Amy's legs. She glanced at Jewel, standing beside her, wide-eyed. Should she tell her to go into the little sewing room to spare her a sight that might frighten her or ask for her help? It took only seconds for her to decide. She was going to need all the help she could get.

"Is it going to be like gross?" Jewel asked.

"Yes," Sofia said. "You don't have to do this, but I could really use your help."

"What do I have to do?"

"Maybe hold her hand. And if I need something, you could run and get it for me."

Jewel gave her a doubtful sidelong look. "Have you ever done this before?"

When it was over, Amy lay back on the pillow holding her baby boy, now wrapped in a blanket, while Jewel sat on the edge of the bed, hardly able to take her eyes off the baby. She had been amazing during the delivery. It turned out Sofia had no reason to worry about her being shocked or repulsed by the experience. She had been at Sofia's side the entire time, ready to bring a washcloth or a bowl of water or anything else Sofia needed.

"What will you call him?" Sofia asked Amy.

"Reuben. That's what Al and I decided on." Amy smiled down at the bundle cradled in her arms. "I can't believe he's really here."

"Do you want me to take him?"

"No, not yet. Let me try to feed him."

Sofia was exhausted. She felt like curling up and taking a nap now that all the excitement was over. She had just stretched out on the floor and closed her eyes, intending to do just that, when Buster barked, startling her. Her first thought was—he'll wake the baby. Her second, that someone was coming. Buster stood by the window, looking out.

Jewel darted to him, knelt, and threw an arm around his neck. "What is it, boy? Do you hear something?"

Now Sofia heard it too. A motor. Faint but unmistakable.

"I see it!" Jewel said.

Sofia jumped up and joined them at the window. A truck was coming up the road. A large black truck. It was still some distance away. She wondered how it could plow through the water so effortlessly. Seconds later she saw how. It rode higher than most trucks, mounted on large tires—a monster truck.

They watched it progress up the road toward them, water spraying up in twin arcs from its tires.

"Should we try to wave it down?" Jewel asked eagerly.

"I don't know," Sofia said. She wasn't sure why she felt reluctant. Something about the truck bothered her. Then she realized what it was. It wasn't stopping to check any houses along the way, just relentlessly advancing. That was odd. Apparently whoever was in it wasn't interested in rescuing people stranded in their homes. They had a destination in mind. Maybe they were owners returning home to check the damage to their property, but whatever their mission, it was odd.

"Shouldn't we wave something to get their attention?" Jewel asked again.

Sofia thought of the sheet still dangling from the window and the sheets she and Jewel had arranged on the roof to spell SOS in case the helicopter returned. If the people in the truck were there to help, surely they would notice these signals.

"I don't think . . ."

The monster truck didn't slow as it passed the turnoff that led to Amy's house.

"The bridge!" Jewel said. "Do you think they'll notice the bridge is out?"

Maybe not. And if the driver of the truck didn't realize the bridge was out, it might go down the same embankment as Jewel's mother had gone down.

"We have to warn them!" Jewel made a dash for the stairs.

It was probably already too late. They would never get to the truck in time.

But Jewel was already pounding down the stairs, and Sofia could not let her go alone. Suppose they were looters? Suppose they were dangerous?

She grabbed her backpack, just in case. She would at least have a gun with her. Then she ran to catch up with Jewel. Buster was standing on the stairway barking as she charged past him. Before she got to the door, she felt the water close around her legs, slowing her down. She pressed on. Once outside, she looked for Jewel. With the heedlessness of the young, the girl was striking out across an open field, no doubt

172

hoping to intercept the truck before it reached the bridge. Sofia had no choice but to follow.

"Wait!" she called out.

Jewel kept going. She was shouting and waving her arms, desperately trying to get the attention of the truck's occupants. But even cutting across the field, she wasn't going to get to the monster truck in time. It was traveling too fast. Sofia felt like she was watching a train wreck take place in slow motion. All she could do was watch helplessly. When the truck came to the curve where the bridge had washed out, the current caught it, and it slowly turned sideways and drifted toward the embankment. A moment later it disappeared over the edge.

At least Jewel had the good sense to veer toward the road and not plunge into the current after it.

She caught up with the girl as she stood on the embankment looking down at the monster truck where it had come to rest next to her mother's SUV. As they watched, the driver's door swung open and a lean man in a baseball cap with a scar on his face climbed out. He wore a white T-shirt with a large image of a fanged snake on the front and the sleeves cut off, baring his heavily tattooed arms. Carlos.

CHAPTER 18

It had finally stopped raining, although the overcast sky made it look as if it might start again at any moment. Not that it mattered much. Mark was thoroughly wet anyway. The floodwater was still more than knee deep, the air humid, and he was sweating. But if it stopped raining, maybe the floodwaters would start to recede. Right now the ground was too saturated to absorb much water, but without more rain eventually the floodwater would drain back into the bay.

As he slogged through the water, he thought about what he would tell Sofia when he saw her again. He wanted to persuade her to come to Denver. It was the only way they would have a chance to get to know each other. If she went to Houston or someplace else, they would just end up going their separate ways, and he would never know what might have been between them.

Of course, Amy would be relieved to hear Al was okay, or alive at any rate and getting the medical attention he needed. Hopefully the baby would hold off its arrival until rescuers got to Amy. In fact, maybe they had already gotten to her, although part of him hoped the women hadn't been rescued yet, because then he might have trouble finding Sofia. He didn't want to lose track of her, but in the aftermath of the storm, it might happen—especially since she was on the run from the police and Carlos Ruiz. If she disappeared, he might not be able to find her again. His fear that he might lose her made him walk faster.

He figured he should be able to get back well before sundown. The main thing was not to get lost. He had Amy's map to guide him, which he only needed to follow in reverse. How hard was that? Besides, he was confident he would remember the houses along the route.

Spending the last twenty-four hours apart from Sofia had given him time to think. As he had told Al, he wanted to help her. He wasn't sure how he could do this, but he would figure it out if she just gave him a chance. Since he had first laid eyes on her that day on the beach, he had hardly stopped thinking about her. And now the prospect of seeing her again made him feel like a giddy teenager.

In all the years he had known Wendy, he had never felt like this about her. Their relationship had just seemed inevitable, like the fact that the sun rose every morning, or that there were twenty-four hours in a day. They had started dating in college and continued while he was in graduate school. When he got the teaching post in Denver, they had decided to move in together and lived together for almost a year. He had been absolutely floored when she announced she had changed her mind about marrying him. He had never seen it coming, although in retrospect maybe he should have. Now he wondered if what had upset him most about the breakup was his fear of how losing her would impact his life and the future he had envisioned for himself—a secure job, a shared circle of friends, a house in a nice neighborhood, kids. When she broke up with him, he was hurt and angry and felt like the bottom had dropped out of his world. Instead, maybe she had done him a favor.

He was near the area where he had rescued the retriever when he heard voices. Not distinct but not too far away either. He stopped to listen, just to be sure. There was a brief silence, and then he heard them again. Men's voices. Yesterday when he had come through here, the area had seemed deserted, but maybe he had missed someone. Although he was eager to get back, what if someone needed help? The voices seemed to be only a little out of his way. He waded toward them. They came and went, but he couldn't make out the words. Then he rounded the corner of a house and saw an inflatable boat tied up to a porch railing several houses away. He hesitated. They could be rescuers. If they were, they didn't need him.

As he watched, two men emerged from the house, one with a scraggly beard wearing a cap, the other clean-shaven and bald. Each carried a bulging black plastic garbage bag, which they slung into the boat. Maybe they were salvaging items from their home or preparing to evacuate someone.

"Hey, everything okay there?" His words rang out across the expanse of water that separated them.

The men looked up, startled, then ducked back in the house without answering. That made him uneasy. Maybe he should just mind his own business. They had a boat. If they needed to evacuate, presumably they could.

A loud bang shattered the silence. A gunshot? Were they shooting at him?

He backed away as quickly as the water would let him. *Looters*, he thought with disgust, and there was nothing he could do to stop them. If they shot him, no one was around to help him. He had the gun in his backpack but no desire to engage in a gunfight with a couple of low-life looters. He'd probably be the one to end up getting shot. And what then? He might bleed to death before anyone found him. And if he never made it back, Sofia would think he had not kept his promise or had a change of heart. She might never know what happened.

In the next few minutes he tried to put as much distance between himself and the looters as he could. When he slowed down and looked around him, he didn't know where he was. And he couldn't backtrack when it might mean running into the men who had shot at him. He consulted Amy's map again, wiping the sweat from his forehead with the back of his arm. If he continued walking in the direction he was going, he should come to the road he and Sofia had been driving on, and then he could follow it south until he came to Al and Amy's house. Once he had decided on this plan, he felt better and resolved to be more careful about approaching strangers. No reason to take stupid risks.

Before long the houses grew farther apart, and he took this as a sign that he was moving away from the city. Then he spotted a road in the distance. Even though it was flooded, he could tell by the broad swath of empty space around it that it was a road. He felt fairly certain that it was the one he and Sofia had been traveling on when her tire blew out and they hit a fence post. The residential areas here gave way to open rural spaces. He had to cross a bridge over a gully swollen with muddy water, but after that he was certain he was headed in the right direction.

Under normal conditions he would have made better time. He watched the houses closely, not wanting to pass Al and Amy's house and end up back at the house where he and Sofia had taken shelter from the storm—or even worse, the police barricade—although surely he would run across Sofia's abandoned pickup before then.

After a while the road ahead curved, and something about the curve made him uneasy. He approached cautiously. As he neared, it hit him what was wrong. A current was flowing across the road. That meant a creek or a stream had overrun its banks. In fact, it looked as if a bridge had washed away. He wondered if this was the same stream he had crossed earlier. If so, he was now on the wrong side of it.

As he stood there debating what to do, his eyes scanning the distance ahead, he realized with excitement that he could see Amy and Al's house in the distance on the other side of the stream. He could just make out the upstairs window with the sheet hanging from it. He was so close and yet cut off by the stream in front of him.

What should he do? He didn't want to get swept away by the current trying to cross. But neither did he want to walk back—maybe an hour's walk—and cross at the bridge over the gully just so he would be on the other side of the stream. He would lose too much time even if it was the safest route. It was already late afternoon, and he didn't want to still be floundering around in floodwater after dark.

As he moved closer, searching for a way to cross, he saw what had happened to an SUV that had tried to cross. It had gone down an embankment and was leaning precariously. He wondered if he could reach the SUV by wading across. It all depended on how deep the water was and how strong the current. Miscalculate and he could get washed away. He stood there a few more minutes trying to make up his mind and then decided to attempt it.

He waded slowly into the current, the water rising until it was up to his chest. He pushed forward against it and for a minute lost his footing and went under, taking in a mouthful of filthy water. When he surfaced, he spit it out and flailed frantically, the backpack and his clothes weighing him down and the current dragging at him. He kept going. Soon he felt the ground under his feet. A moment later he grasped the front bumper of the SUV and knew he had made it to the other side. He looked through the windshield of the SUV and saw a woman's face. Her half-open unblinking eyes told him she was dead.

Before he could climb the embankment, he heard the roar of an engine approaching, moving fast. He just had time to duck behind the SUV before a huge black pickup truck came sliding over the embankment, nose down.

CHAPTER 19

When Carlos stepped out of the monster truck, Sofia stared at him in shock. She wasn't sure what she had expected but certainly not Carlos.

If he was surprised to see her, he didn't show it.

"Hi ya, babe," he said, as if he drove monster trucks off bridges every day. He lifted his baseball cap and wiped the sweat off his forehead with the back of his arm.

"What are you doing here?" she asked.

"I'm here to take you home." He looked down at the water he stood in and then around them at the flat land that stretched away like a shallow lake with trees growing in it.

To take her home? What made him think she would go with him? And how did he intend to take anybody anywhere when the truck he had been driving was practically submerged in the swollen stream? Unless he could get it back up the embankment, he was just as much in need of rescue as she was.

"How did you know where to find me?"

He shifted from one leg to the other. "A little bird told me."

She knew who told him. Gomez and Ramos. Or that tracker he had put under her pickup.

"Where'd you get the truck?"

"Borrowed it. From a friend."

Or was it stolen? Best not to ask. Don't say anything that might antagonize him.

She couldn't tell from looking at him if he was still mad at her, but in any case she didn't intend to go anywhere with him. Had he forgotten that he had set the cops on her? If he got her back home, he would probably beat her. He never forgot or forgave when someone crossed him. She must not make the mistake of thinking she was the exception.

"Who's the kid?" he asked, still standing next to the truck looking up at her as if he had not quite made up his mind to climb the embankment.

Every muscle froze. She had forgotten Jewel standing beside her. Alarm bells went off in her head. She had to protect the girl from him and all the darkness that swirled around him. If only she and Jewel had not gone running after the truck! She should have listened to the inner voice that warned her to stay where she was. Now she must think fast if she wanted to keep Jewel safe.

"That's my mother down there," Jewel said in a clear piping voice, pointing.

Just when Sofia wanted her to be invisible, she had to open her mouth and draw attention to herself.

Carlos glanced back at the white SUV. "Yeah?"

She had to keep Jewel from telling him anything more. In fact, she had to get rid of him. They couldn't take him back to the house. It would be dangerous for Amy and the baby. Dangerous for all of them.

"Do you think you can get your truck back on the road?" she asked, trying to keep her voice carefully neutral. If he could get it back on the road, maybe she could persuade him to go away.

"Maybe. But I'm not leaving here without you."

"I'm not going with you." Important that he understand that. She had to stand her ground.

"Sure you are."

A movement behind him caught her eye as someone stepped out from behind the white SUV. Mark. She stared. What was *he* doing here? Her mind raced, trying to make sense of it.

"You heard her," Mark said. "She's not going anywhere with you."

Carlos whirled about in surprise. "Where'd you come from?"

She wanted to know that too, but there was no time for explanations. Suddenly Carlos had a gun in his hand. He must have pulled it from his belt. Her arm shot out protectively, warning Jewel to step back.

"Wait," she said. "I'll go with you." The gun changed everything. She didn't want anyone to get hurt. Agreeing to go with him was the only way she could think of to defuse the situation.

"No," Mark said. "You can't."

Just once couldn't he think about self-preservation? If Carlos shot at that range, he didn't stand a chance.

"Don't shoot," she said to Carlos. "I'll go with you."

But he wasn't listening. His attention was all on Mark now.

"You really have a knack for sticking your nose in where it doesn't belong. You should have left when you had the chance."

"You think shooting me is going to solve anything?" Mark said.

"Yeah, I do."

"*Just stop!*" She yanked the backpack off her back, plunged her hand into it, and pulled out the gun she had stashed there. She aimed it at Carlos and released the safety.

"Babe, you're not going to shoot me," he said, his gun never wavering from Mark.

"Jewel, get out of here," she said.

The girl took a few steps backward, not nearly as many as Sofia had in mind.

She didn't want to shoot Carlos, but she would if she had to. And she knew wounding him wouldn't stop him. It would just make him madder. If she shot, she had to shoot to kill.

"Why can't you leave me alone?" she cried.

There was a loud crack as his gun fired.

She watched in horror as Mark staggered back, clutching his chest. Behind her Jewel screamed. She shot before Carlos could shoot again. And then she scrambled down the embankment, her heart pounding, floundering through the water to Mark first, who was clinging to the SUV bumper with one hand and clutching his chest with the other. His face had a look of disbelief.

At least he was alive.

"I have to tell you—" His voice sounded strained.

"Not now. Can you walk?" All she could think about was how to get him up the embankment. If he passed out, she wasn't sure she could drag him up even with Jewel's help. And if he stayed down here, she was afraid he would die.

Jewel came splashing up beside her. "You shot him," she said, her eyes wide as she looked at where Carlos had slipped under the water.

"Here, can you keep him from going under?" Sofia said, handing off Mark to the girl. "I need to check—" The words choked in her throat. She waded to Carlos and pulled him upright so his face wasn't under water. With shaking fingers, she felt for a pulse in his neck and couldn't find one. She had never killed anyone before. She felt like throwing up. Another sin to atone for, this one worse than any she had committed so far. He may have done bad things, but he had helped her and in his own twisted way he had loved her.

"Is he dead?" Jewel asked.

"I think so."

There wasn't anything they could do for Carlos, so they left him there, propped against one of the enormous tires of the monster truck. She draped Mark's arm around her neck and helped him stagger up the embankment. Jewel followed with his backpack.

She worried how they would get him back to the house. It seemed so far away and he was bleeding. She was afraid he would pass out.

"I have to tell you—" he said, his voice sounding strained.

"Save your breath. Wait till we get back to the house."

"No, now," he insisted stubbornly.

"You're *not* going to die," she said fiercely. Not if she could help it. She had lost too many people already. Etched in her mind was the image of Hector bleeding out on the pavement in front of that little grocery store, dying from a bullet intended for someone else. He had just been unlucky enough to get in the way. She had come so far to get away from violence and here it was again.

Mark tried to grin but it was more a grimace. "Don't intend to."

"What were you doing down there anyway?" she demanded, her voice harsher than she intended. She meant why was he hiding behind the white SUV.

"On my way back," he said, his breath ragged.

That made no sense. He was coming from the wrong direction. North. He should have been coming from the east. How had he ended up on the road where the bridge was washed out? She told herself it didn't matter now. All that mattered was to get him back to the house.

"Tell Amy—"

Her blood ran cold. She froze. She had completely forgotten about Al. "Tell Amy what?"

"Al's okay."

Relief swept over her and she started walking again. "You can tell her yourself."

"Want you to know. I love you. Should've said it sooner."

"Don't talk. Save your strength."

"Want to marry you." He slurred the words.

She stared straight ahead. He had just got shot because of her. Did he have to say that *now*? Was he trying to break her heart into a million pieces?

Jewel sidled up next to her. "Did he just propose to you?"

It seemed to take forever to get him back to the house. They put one foot in front of the other and slowly made their way across the flooded field. He was heavier than she would have thought. Even if they hadn't been trudging through water over uneven ground, it would have been hard.

"Let me explain to Amy what happened," she told Jewel before they got to the house. She didn't want Jewel to upset Amy by blurting out that she had killed a man.

"Can I tell her about Al?" Jewel asked.

"Yes, you can tell her about Al."

By now they had been gone so long that Amy would be worried about them. Jewel, impatient, forged ahead with the news that Al was injured but safe. Sofia and Mark progressed at a slower pace until at last they mounted the steps to the porch. Once they were inside, getting him up the stairs was another challenge. There was a bannister to hold onto, but the stairs were narrow for two abreast.

When they made it to the top of the stairs, she wondered where to put him. Amy was lying on the bed in the master bedroom with the baby, so they couldn't put him there.

"What happened?" Amy said when she caught sight of them in the doorway. The front of Mark's T-shirt was soaked with blood and blood stained the front of Sofia's T-shirt too.

They probably looked as if they had wandered out of a slasher movie.

"He had an accident," Sofia said. "Let me just find a place to lay him down."

"What kind of accident?"

"I'll explain later."

"Okay. There's a sleeper sofa in the next room."

"I'll help," Jewel said.

Soon they had the sleeper sofa open and old blankets laid down so Mark wouldn't bleed all over everything. After cutting away his T-shirt with a pair of scissors, Sofia did her best to wash his wound and dress it. It was near his left shoulder. He had been lucky, or maybe Carlos intended just to wound him with the first shot. She had managed to get the bleeding stopped, but he would need a doctor to remove the bullet.

Propped up by a couple of pillows, he watched her as she patched him up. Jewel, with Buster at her heels, ducked in and out of the room, curious to see what she was doing, then wrinkling her nose in disgust and retreating, only to return a few minutes later.

"Does it hurt?" Sofia asked as she added one more strip of tape over the gauze that covered his wound.

"Only when I breathe."

She rolled her eyes. "You should have just stayed out of sight."

"I thought you needed help."

"Well, I didn't. I had everything under control."

"I didn't want you to go with him."

"I wouldn't have. I told you. I can take care of myself."

"What I said before—about marrying you. I meant it."

"Don't. Not right now. You don't know what you're saying."

"Yes, I do. Listen, I had a lot of time out there to think about it. Carlos Ruiz was not the first person to take a shot at me today." He held up a hand to keep her from interrupting. "I got to thinking how life can be over in an instant."

He looked so vulnerable sitting there with his chest wound bandaged. Of course, she knew life could be over in an instant. One minute you could be shopping for groceries with your family and the next you could be lying on the pavement bleeding to death. She didn't need anyone explaining to her how fast everything could be taken away from you.

He was watching her face. "What? You don't want to marry me? If that's it, just say so. I'll understand."

"It's not that simple."

"Why not?"

"Because I just killed someone." There, she had said it. Not just killed someone. Killed Carlos, who had helped her cross the border with Diego. Carlos, with whom she had shared a bed for the past nine months. This was how she had repaid him. She had had no choice, yet how would she ever forgive herself?

"You saved my life," he said, reaching for her hand.

"But I doubt the police will see it that way. I could go to prison. At the very least, I'll be deported."

"I'll say I did it."

She shook her head. "You can't take the blame for what I did. It wouldn't be right. Besides, no one would believe it."

"I'll say it was self-defense."

"I can't let you do that."

"Why not? You think they're going to send me to prison for killing a man like Ruiz?"

Maybe not, but she still couldn't let him take the blame for what she had done.

"There's one more thing," he said. "I'm not Catholic. In fact, I'm not even much of a believer. Will that be a problem?"

A problem? *That* was what he was worried about? Did he think she didn't know?

"You don't understand," she said. "I'm not free to marry."

"What do you mean?"

"There's something I have to do first."

"I know. Find Diego."

Tears sprang to her eyes. He had guessed right. Much as she wanted to be with him, she knew she couldn't be happy while Diego was missing. There would be a hole in her heart until she found him. She had given up her country. She had given up everything she knew. She had come all this way to a country that didn't want her. She could not give up Diego too.

"I'll help find him," he said, squeezing her hand.

She looked at him through her tears. Was his heart big enough to love her son too and be a father to him? Because she would not allow herself any other kind of love.

In the distance she heard the deep blast of a horn. An odd sound, not like a car horn.

Jewel bounded into the room. "You have to see this," she said, rushing to the window and raising it.

Sofia rose and crossed the room to join her. Against the setting sun a flotilla of small craft was swarming up the flooded road—inflatables, rowboats, an airboat, a canoe, and several kayaks.

"We're going to be rescued," Jewel said.

CHAPTER 20
Nine months later

They sat together in a room at a courthouse in Denver with other parents. Sofia was wearing a new flowered dress and sandals, and Mark was wearing a white shirt and a tie. He reached over and squeezed her hand.

"It will be okay," he said as he had half a dozen times already.

She nodded but still looked worried. She was waiting to see Diego for the first time in a year and a half.

Finding him had taken the combined efforts of scores of people and dozens of organizations, and at times she had feared she might never see him again. Al had advised her how to seek legal help in her search for Diego. She'd had no idea there were so many people dedicated to helping parents like her who had been separated from their children, and she had been shocked to find out how many other parents were searching for their children too. The practice of separating children from migrant parents was no longer a closely guarded secret but a national scandal that had been covered by news agencies around the world. Her heart ached for the parents of the children still missing. No one seemed to know how many of them there were. Thankfully Diego was no longer among them.

After several false leads and dead ends, he had finally been found living with a foster family in Milwaukee, a city in the Midwest she had never heard of before. When she was first told, she wanted to drop everything and rush there at once. Only after much persuasion did she agree to wait for the courts to do their work and return him to her.

Her life had changed so much in the past nine months. She and Mark were married now and lived in a small house with a fenced-in backyard in a Denver suburb. She was training to be a docent at the Denver Art Museum and enrolled in a night class in citizenship at a nearby high school. Since moving to Denver, she had become friends with Eric's widow Terry and, like Mark, grown fond of her sons, Noah and Jacob.

She and Mark had been back to Corpus Christi several times—once to attend an exhibition of Jackie's paintings and another to attend a reading by Cat of her latest novel. She felt fortunate to be a friend of both women and proud of their success. It still startled her to see her own face looking out from several of Jackie's canvases, but it secretly pleased her too.

On one of their visits they had stopped by the old Spanish church to see Father Angelo, and they had gone back to the beach on Mustang Island where they first met. The Gulf was what she missed most—the smell of saltwater, the blue expanse of water, the wind in her hair, sand powdering her skin, and the cries of the gulls.

Before they had left Texas, she had told the police how she had seen Carlos stab Eric while he was tied to a chair at La Roca. They had recovered his body after the hurricane when it had washed ashore on Mustang Island.

In the end they had not charged her with the death of Carlos Ruiz, and for that she was grateful. She was still waiting to find out if she would be granted asylum, but Al thought she had a good case.

She looked down at Mark's hand holding hers. He caught her eye and smiled. She knew Diego would have changed. He was a year and a half older now. She worried that he wouldn't remember her. And even if he did, after so long he might resent being taken away from his foster family.

There were about twenty parents in the room, some couples, some alone, some with relatives, all looking just as anxious as she felt. They whispered to each other in low voices. Sometimes another mother's eyes met hers and they exchanged nervous smiles.

Finally the door they had all been watching opened and an immaculately groomed young woman in a dark pantsuit led in a dozen children of different heights, some clutching stuffed toys or small bundles of possessions. Sofia's heart leaped into her throat and she stood. More than a year had passed since she had last seen him and he had grown so much, but she would have recognized him anywhere. The same curve of his cheek, the same half-parted lips, the same serious expression. She pressed her fist to her mouth to stifle a sob and then threw open her arms.

"Diego," she said.

He looked at her, hesitated for the briefest of moments, then flew into her arms.

She told him in Spanish she had missed him so much, but the blank look on his face stopped her.

She switched to English.

"I've missed you so much! My how you've grown!"

He stared at Mark. She had imagined this moment so many times. How to explain to him? She took a deep breath.

"This is Mark. He's going to be your new daddy."

"Hi, Diego," Mark said, holding out a hand.

The boy lowered his head shyly, staring at his feet. It would take time, she told herself. They would all have some adjusting to do.

"My name is David now," he said in a voice barely above a whisper. He looked up at her with those beautiful long-lashed dark eyes she remembered so well and put his small hand in hers.

She could have wept. "Your name can be whatever you want it to be," she said. "Shall we go home now?"

ABOUT THE AUTHOR

DEANNA MADDEN has taught literature and creative writing at colleges on the U.S. mainland and in Hawaii. She is the author of *Helena Landless*, *Gaslight and Fog*, *The Wall*, *Forbidden Places*, *The World Beyond: A Novel of Ancient Greece*, and *The Box*. She lives in Honolulu with her family.